16 -

STONE ARCH BOOKS
a capstone imprint

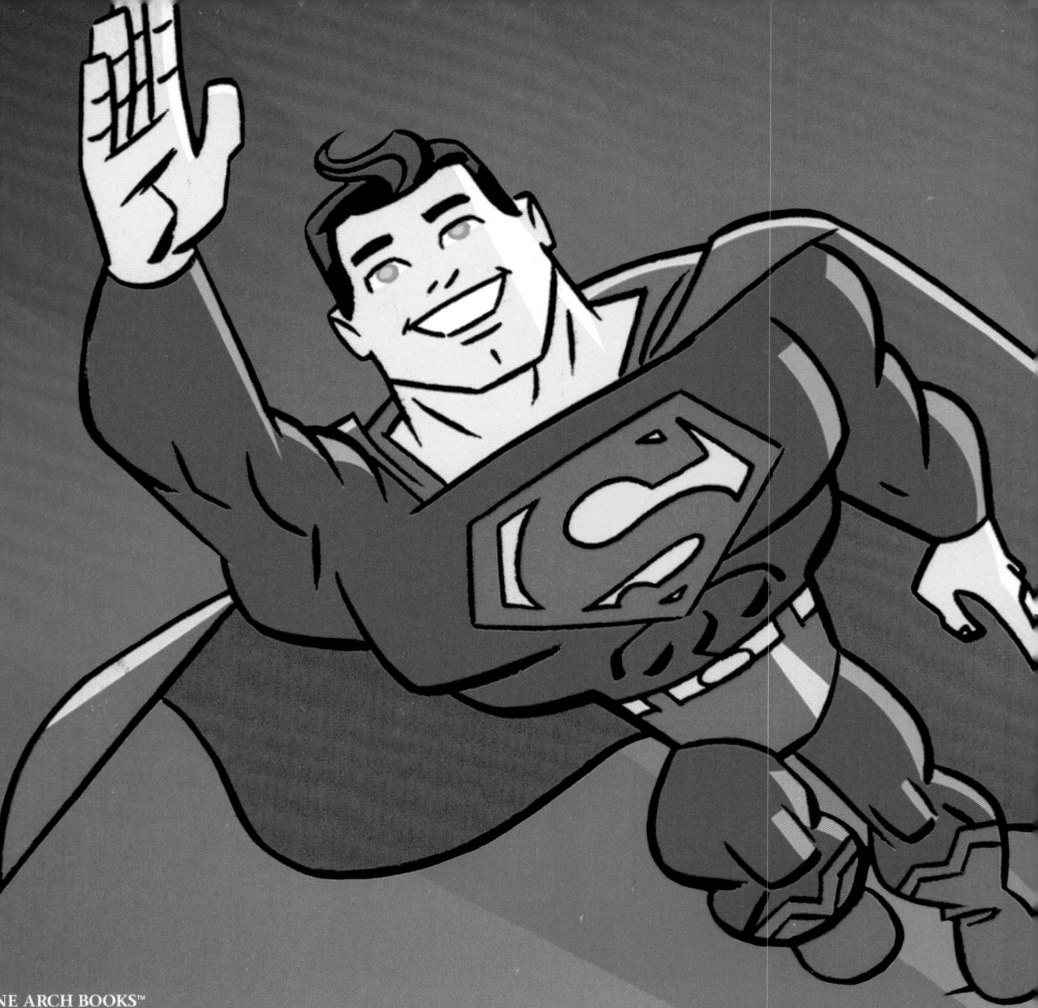

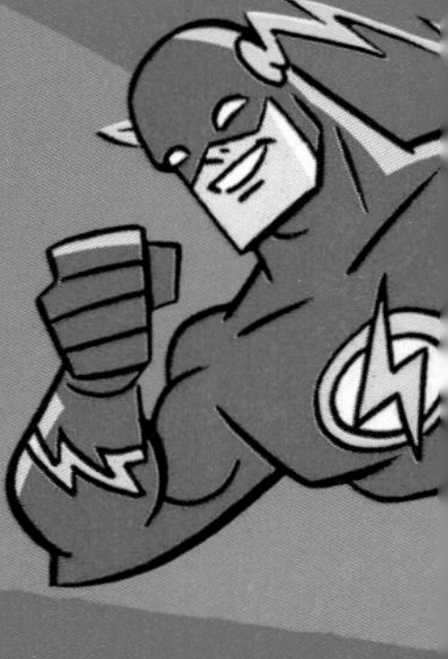

STONE ARCH BOOKS™
Published in 2012
A Capstone Imprint
1710 Roe Crest Drive
North Mankato, MN 56003
www.capstonepub.com

Originally published by DC Comics in
the U.S. in single magazine form as
DC Super Friends #1.


Cataloging-in-Publication Data is available at the
Library of Congress website:
ISBN: 978-1-4342-4541-0 (library binding)

Summary: The World's Greatest Super Heroes are
here to save the day - and be your friends, too!
Follow along as they defend Earth against Amazo,
the android who has all the same powers as Batman,
Superman, and the other Super Friends.

*STONE ARCH BOOKS*
Ashley C. Andersen Zantop *Publisher*
Michael Dahl *Editorial Director*
Donald Lemke & Julie Gassman *Editors*
Heather Kindseth *Creative Director*
Brann Garvey *Designer*
Kathy McColley *Production Specialist*

*DC COMICS*
Rachel Gluckstern *Original U.S. Editor*

Printed in the United States of America
in Brainerd, Minnesota.
032012 006672BANGF12



DC Comics
1700 Broadway, New York, NY 10019
A Warner Bros. Entertainment Company

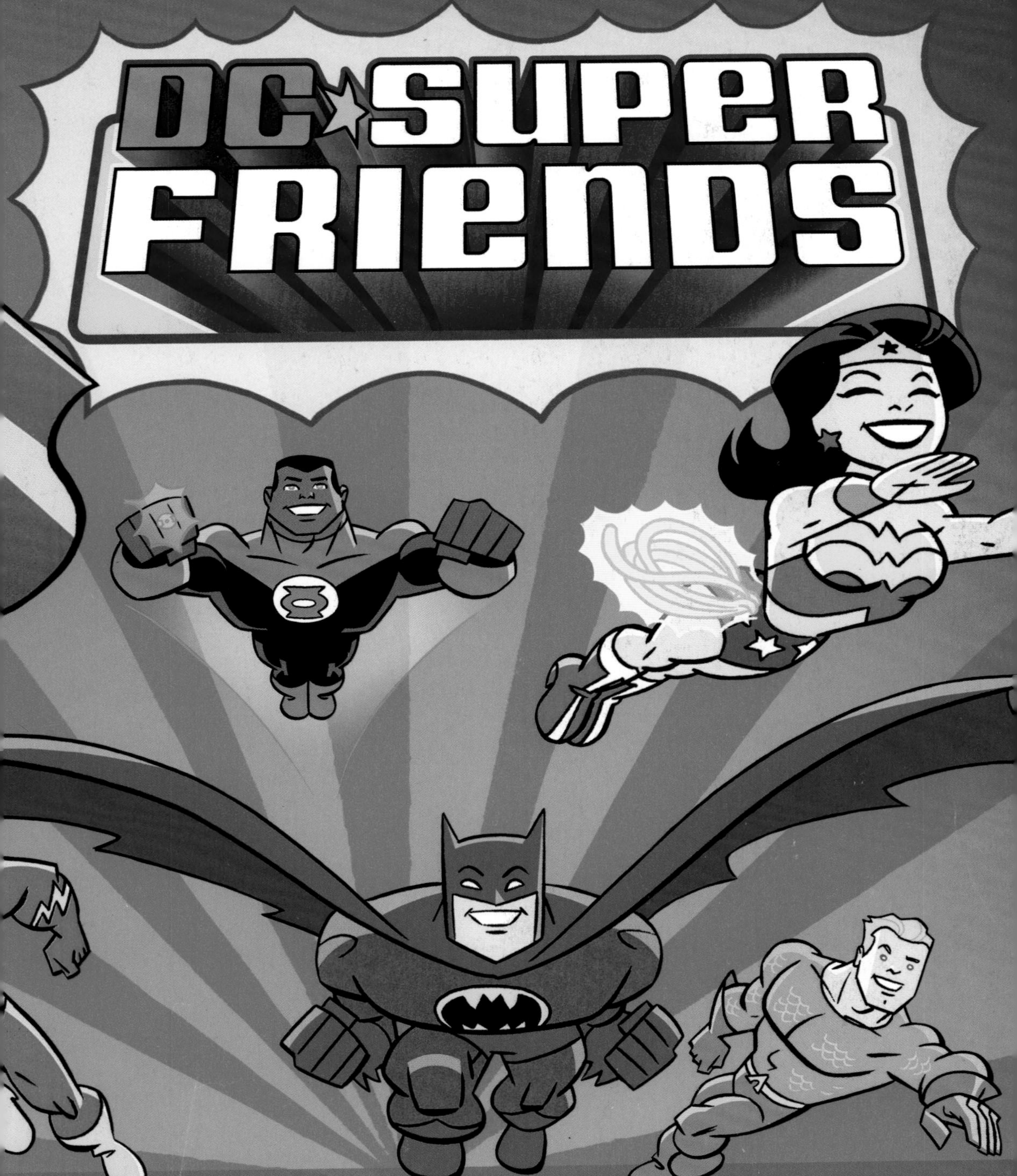
DC SUPER FRIENDS

# HUNGRY FOR POWER

Sholly Fisch ........................... writer
Dario Brizuela......................... artist
Heroic Age ........................... colorist
Rob Clark, Jr. ...................... letters
J. Bone ......................... cover artist

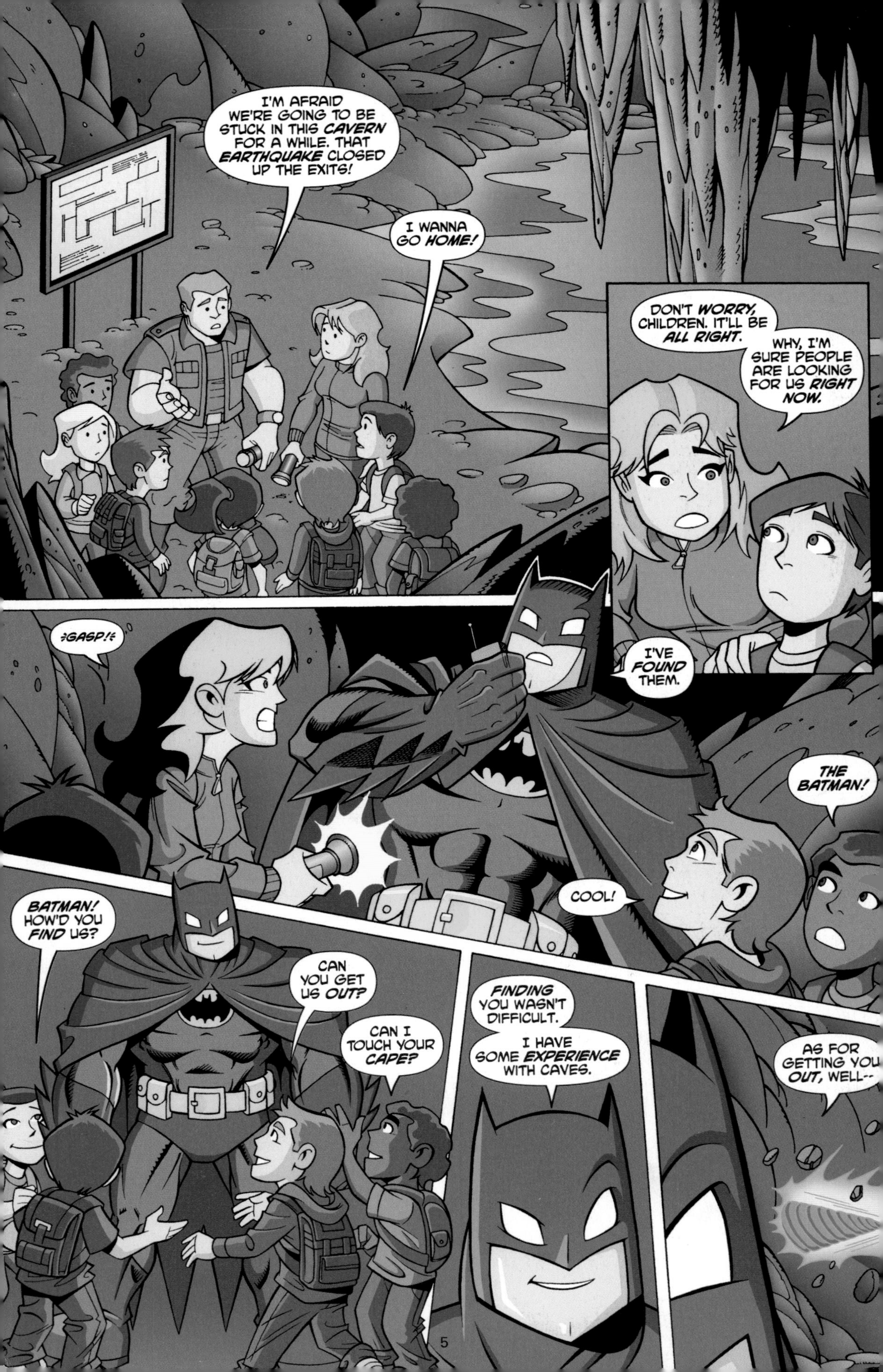
I'M AFRAID WE'RE GOING TO BE STUCK IN THIS *CAVERN* FOR A WHILE. THAT *EARTHQUAKE* CLOSED UP THE EXITS!
I WANNA GO *HOME!*
DON'T *WORRY,* CHILDREN. IT'LL BE *ALL RIGHT.*
WHY, I'M SURE PEOPLE ARE LOOKING FOR US *RIGHT NOW.*
*GASP!*
I'VE *FOUND* THEM.
*THE BATMAN!*
COOL!
*BATMAN!* HOW'D YOU *FIND* US?
CAN YOU GET US *OUT?*
CAN I TOUCH YOUR *CAPE?*
*FINDING* YOU WASN'T DIFFICULT.
I HAVE SOME *EXPERIENCE* WITH CAVES.
AS FOR GETTING YOU *OUT,* WELL--

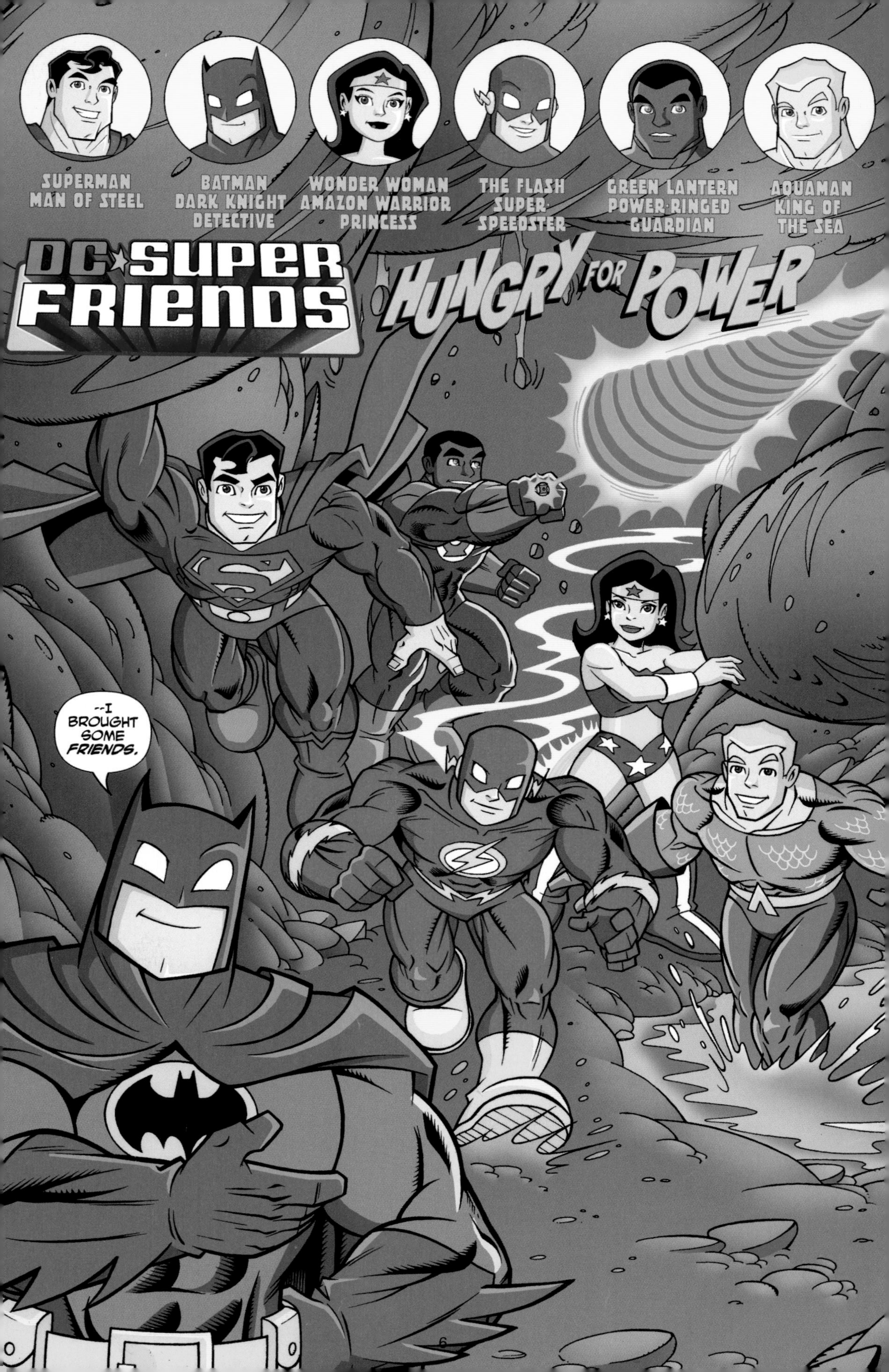
SUPERMAN
MAN OF STEEL
BATMAN
DARK KNIGHT DETECTIVE
WONDER WOMAN
AMAZON WARRIOR PRINCESS
THE FLASH
SUPER-SPEEDSTER
GREEN LANTERN
POWER-RINGED GUARDIAN
AQUAMAN
KING OF THE SEA
DC SUPER FRIENDS
HUNGRY FOR POWER
--I BROUGHT SOME FRIENDS.

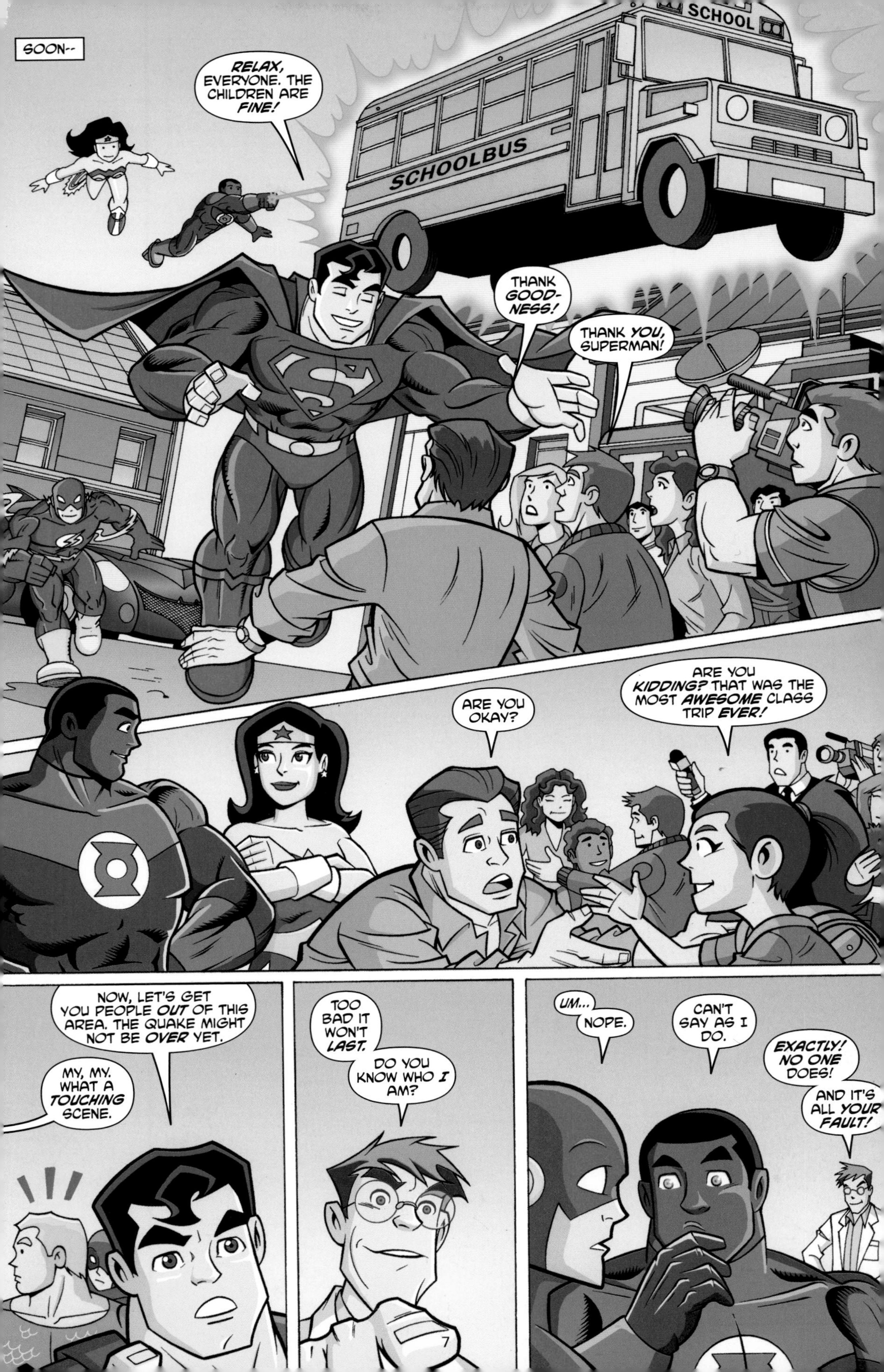
SOON--
RELAX, EVERYONE. THE CHILDREN ARE FINE!
SCHOOL
SCHOOLBUS
THANK GOOD-NESS!
THANK YOU, SUPERMAN!
ARE YOU OKAY?
ARE YOU KIDDING? THAT WAS THE MOST AWESOME CLASS TRIP EVER!
NOW, LET'S GET YOU PEOPLE OUT OF THIS AREA. THE QUAKE MIGHT NOT BE OVER YET.
MY, MY. WHAT A TOUCHING SCENE.
TOO BAD IT WON'T LAST.
DO YOU KNOW WHO I AM?
UM...
NOPE.
CAN'T SAY AS I DO.
EXACTLY! NO ONE DOES!
AND IT'S ALL YOUR FAULT!

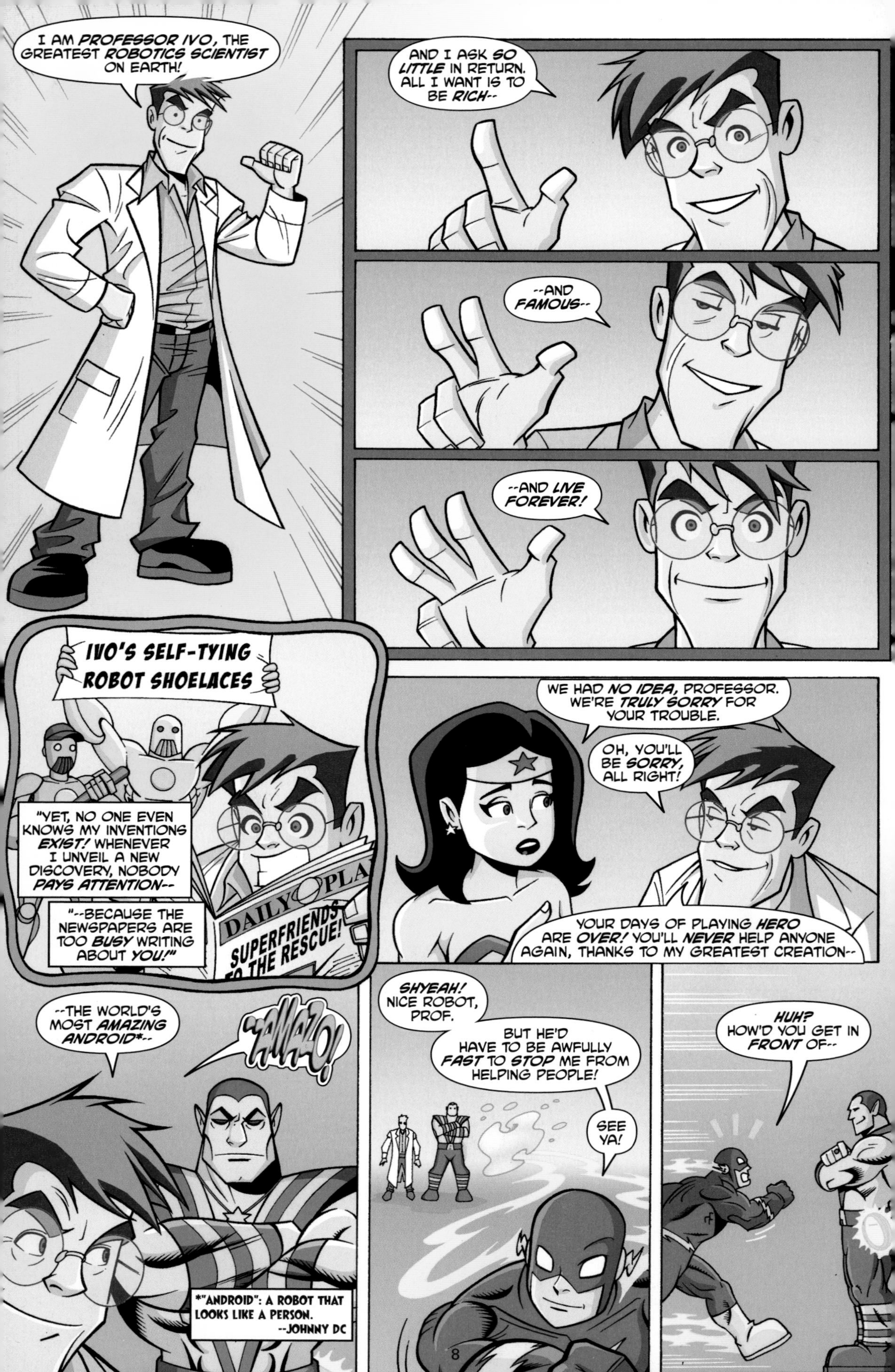
I AM PROFESSOR IVO, THE GREATEST ROBOTICS SCIENTIST ON EARTH!
AND I ASK SO LITTLE IN RETURN. ALL I WANT IS TO BE RICH--
--AND FAMOUS--
--AND LIVE FOREVER!
IVO'S SELF-TYING ROBOT SHOELACES
"YET, NO ONE EVEN KNOWS MY INVENTIONS EXIST! WHENEVER I UNVEIL A NEW DISCOVERY, NOBODY PAYS ATTENTION--
"--BECAUSE THE NEWSPAPERS ARE TOO BUSY WRITING ABOUT YOU!"
DAILY PLA
SUPERFRIENDS TO THE RESCUE!
WE HAD NO IDEA, PROFESSOR. WE'RE TRULY SORRY FOR YOUR TROUBLE.
OH, YOU'LL BE SORRY, ALL RIGHT!
YOUR DAYS OF PLAYING HERO ARE OVER! YOU'LL NEVER HELP ANYONE AGAIN, THANKS TO MY GREATEST CREATION--
--THE WORLD'S MOST AMAZING ANDROID*--
"AMAZO!"
*"ANDROID": A ROBOT THAT LOOKS LIKE A PERSON. --JOHNNY DC
SHYEAH! NICE ROBOT, PROF.
BUT HE'D HAVE TO BE AWFULLY FAST TO STOP ME FROM HELPING PEOPLE!
SEE YA!
HUH? HOW'D YOU GET IN FRONT OF--

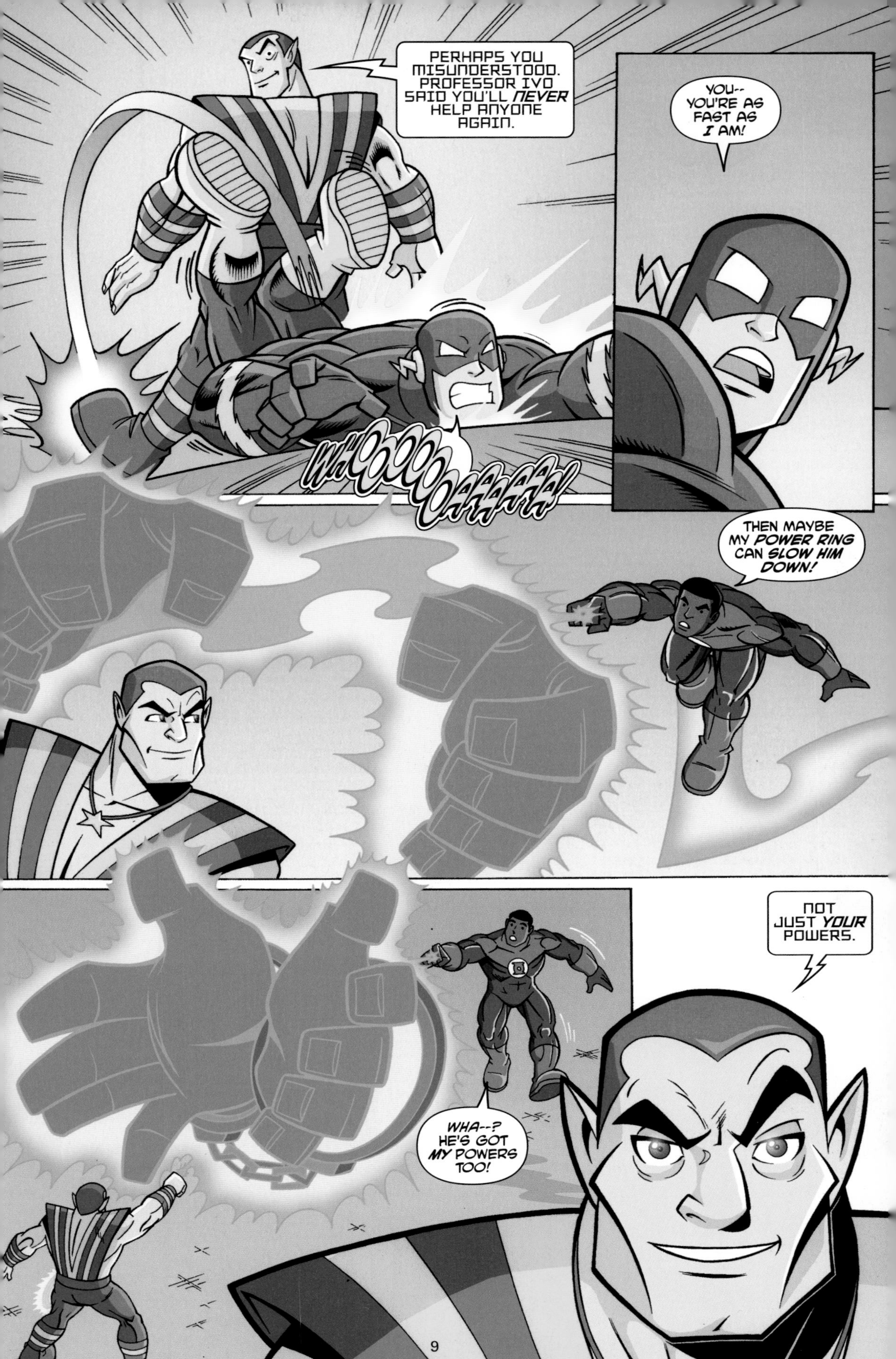
PERHAPS YOU MISUNDERSTOOD. PROFESSOR IVO SAID YOU'LL NEVER HELP ANYONE AGAIN.
WHOOOOOOAAAAAA!
YOU-- YOU'RE AS FAST AS I AM!
THEN MAYBE MY POWER RING CAN SLOW HIM DOWN!
NOT JUST YOUR POWERS.
WHA--? HE'S GOT MY POWERS TOO!

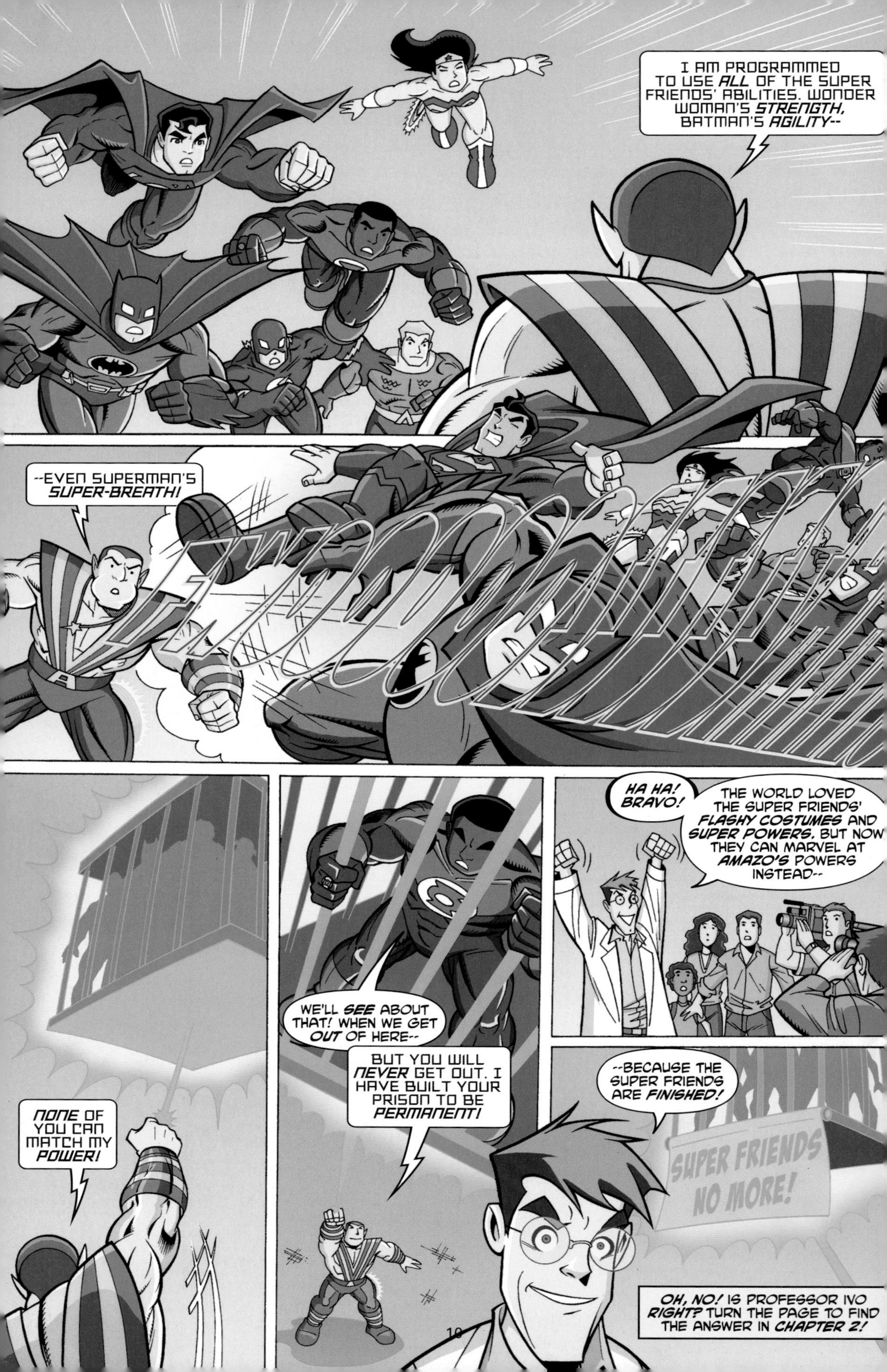

I AM PROGRAMMED TO USE ALL OF THE SUPER FRIENDS' ABILITIES. WONDER WOMAN'S STRENGTH, BATMAN'S AGILITY--
--EVEN SUPERMAN'S SUPER-BREATH!
NONE OF YOU CAN MATCH MY POWER!
WE'LL SEE ABOUT THAT! WHEN WE GET OUT OF HERE--
BUT YOU WILL NEVER GET OUT. I HAVE BUILT YOUR PRISON TO BE PERMANENT!
HA HA! BRAVO!
THE WORLD LOVED THE SUPER FRIENDS' FLASHY COSTUMES AND SUPER POWERS. BUT NOW THEY CAN MARVEL AT AMAZO'S POWERS INSTEAD--
--BECAUSE THE SUPER FRIENDS ARE FINISHED!
SUPER FRIENDS NO MORE!
OH, NO! IS PROFESSOR IVO RIGHT? TURN THE PAGE TO FIND THE ANSWER IN CHAPTER 2!

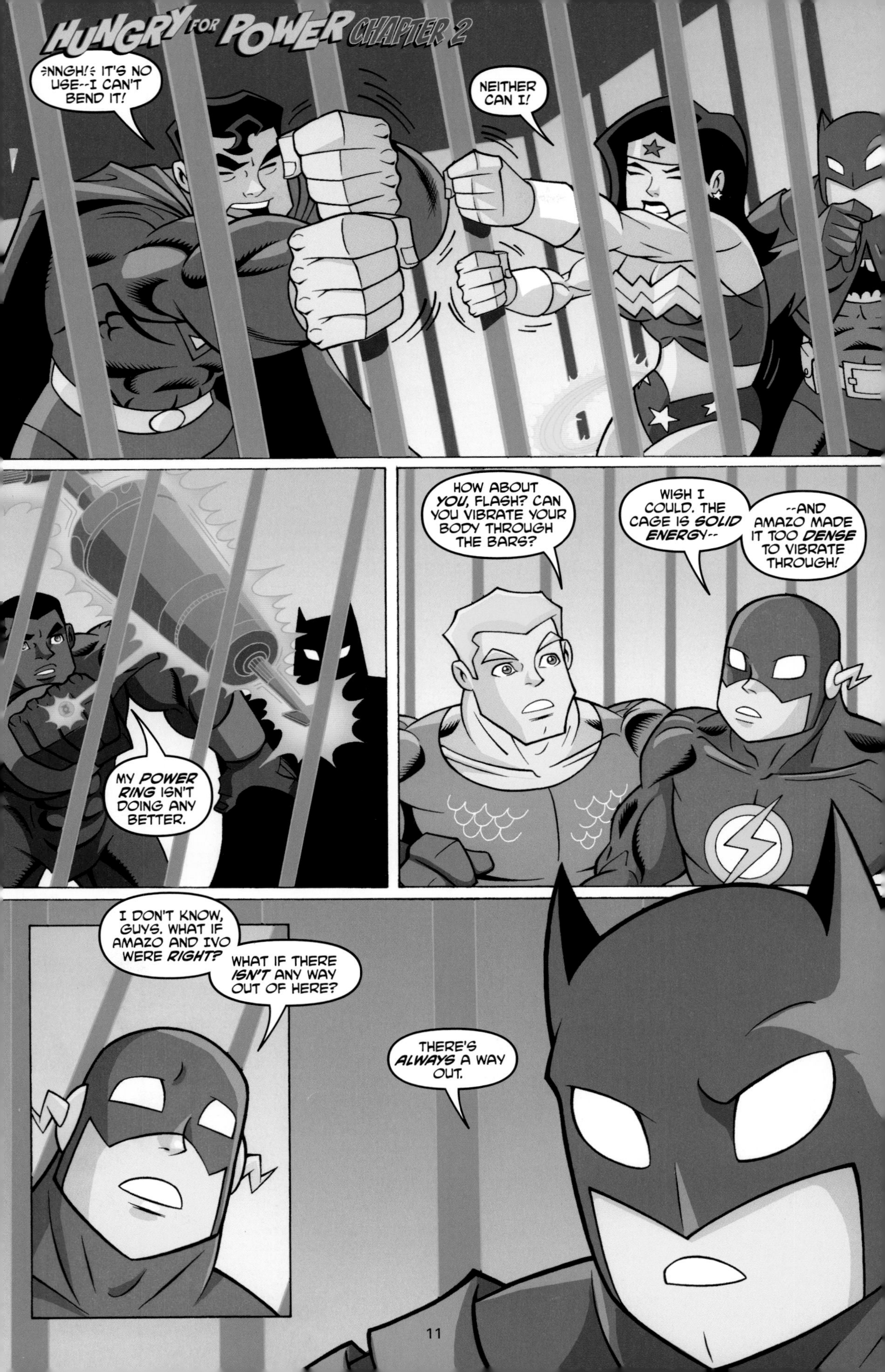
HUNGRY FOR POWER CHAPTER 2
≡NNGH!≡ IT'S NO USE--I CAN'T BEND IT!
NEITHER CAN I!
MY POWER RING ISN'T DOING ANY BETTER.
HOW ABOUT YOU, FLASH? CAN YOU VIBRATE YOUR BODY THROUGH THE BARS?
WISH I COULD. THE CAGE IS SOLID ENERGY--
--AND AMAZO MADE IT TOO DENSE TO VIBRATE THROUGH!
I DON'T KNOW, GUYS. WHAT IF AMAZO AND IVO WERE RIGHT?
WHAT IF THERE ISN'T ANY WAY OUT OF HERE?
THERE'S ALWAYS A WAY OUT.

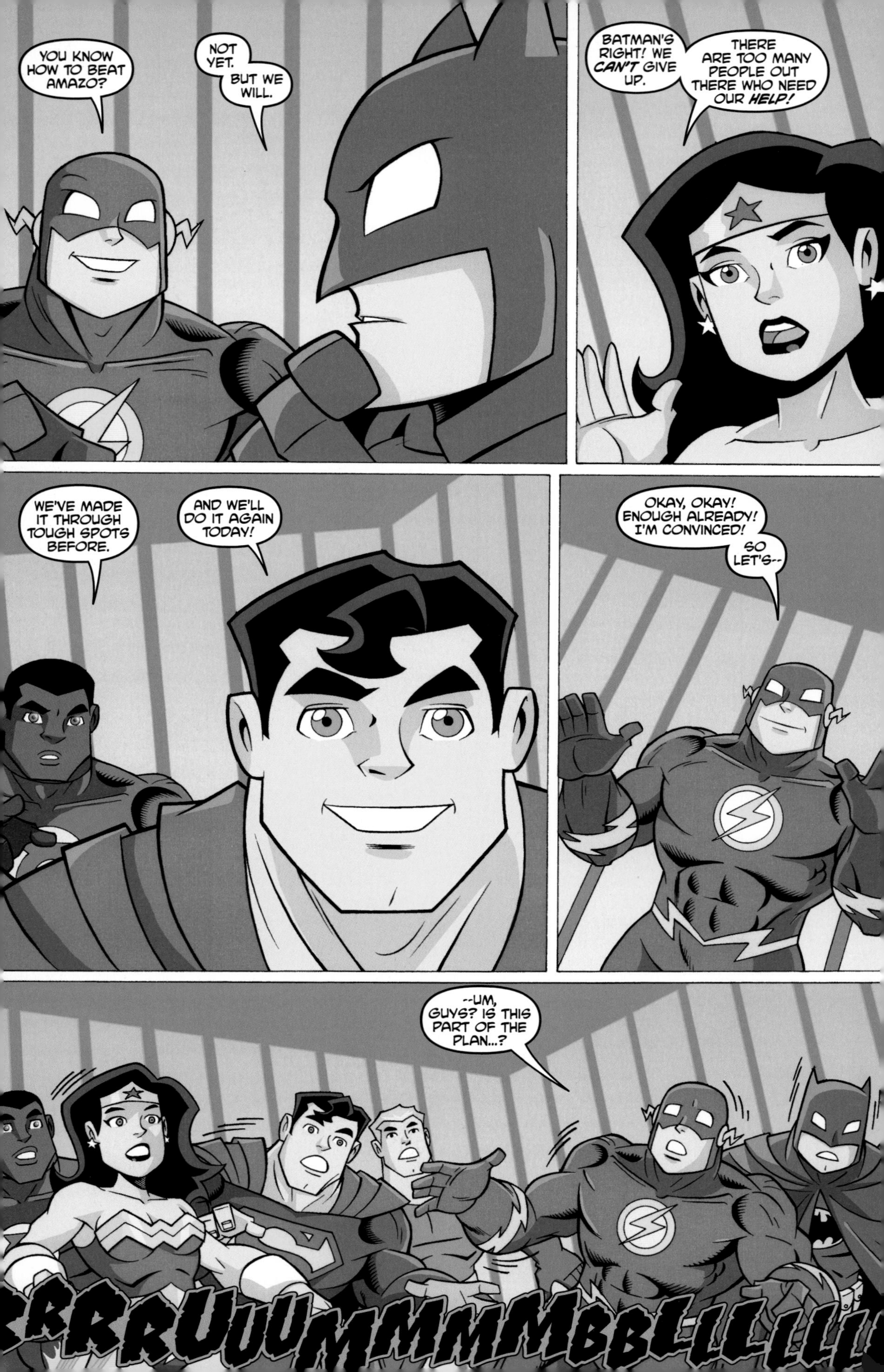
YOU KNOW HOW TO BEAT AMAZO?
NOT YET.
BUT WE WILL.
BATMAN'S RIGHT! WE *CAN'T* GIVE UP.
THERE ARE TOO MANY PEOPLE OUT THERE WHO NEED OUR ***HELP!***
WE'VE MADE IT THROUGH TOUGH SPOTS BEFORE.
AND WE'LL DO IT AGAIN TODAY!
OKAY, OKAY! ENOUGH ALREADY! I'M CONVINCED!
SO LET'S--
--UM, GUYS? IS THIS PART OF THE PLAN...?
KRRRUUUMMMMMBBLLLLL!!

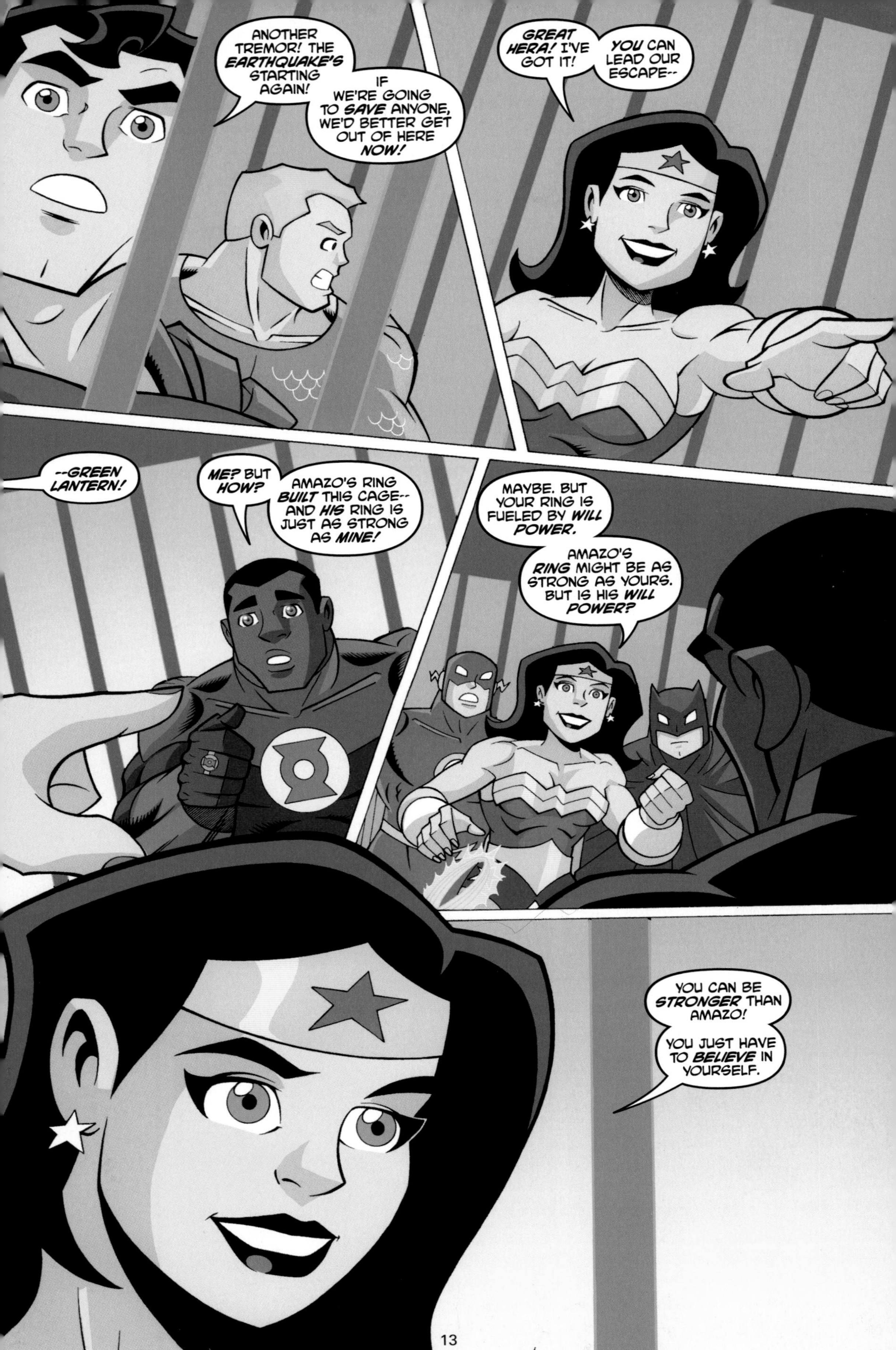
ANOTHER TREMOR! THE EARTHQUAKE'S STARTING AGAIN!
IF WE'RE GOING TO SAVE ANYONE, WE'D BETTER GET OUT OF HERE NOW!
GREAT HERA! I'VE GOT IT!
YOU CAN LEAD OUR ESCAPE--
--GREEN LANTERN!
ME? BUT HOW?
AMAZO'S RING BUILT THIS CAGE-- AND HIS RING IS JUST AS STRONG AS MINE!
MAYBE. BUT YOUR RING IS FUELED BY WILL POWER.
AMAZO'S RING MIGHT BE AS STRONG AS YOURS. BUT IS HIS WILL POWER?
YOU CAN BE STRONGER THAN AMAZO!
YOU JUST HAVE TO BELIEVE IN YOURSELF.

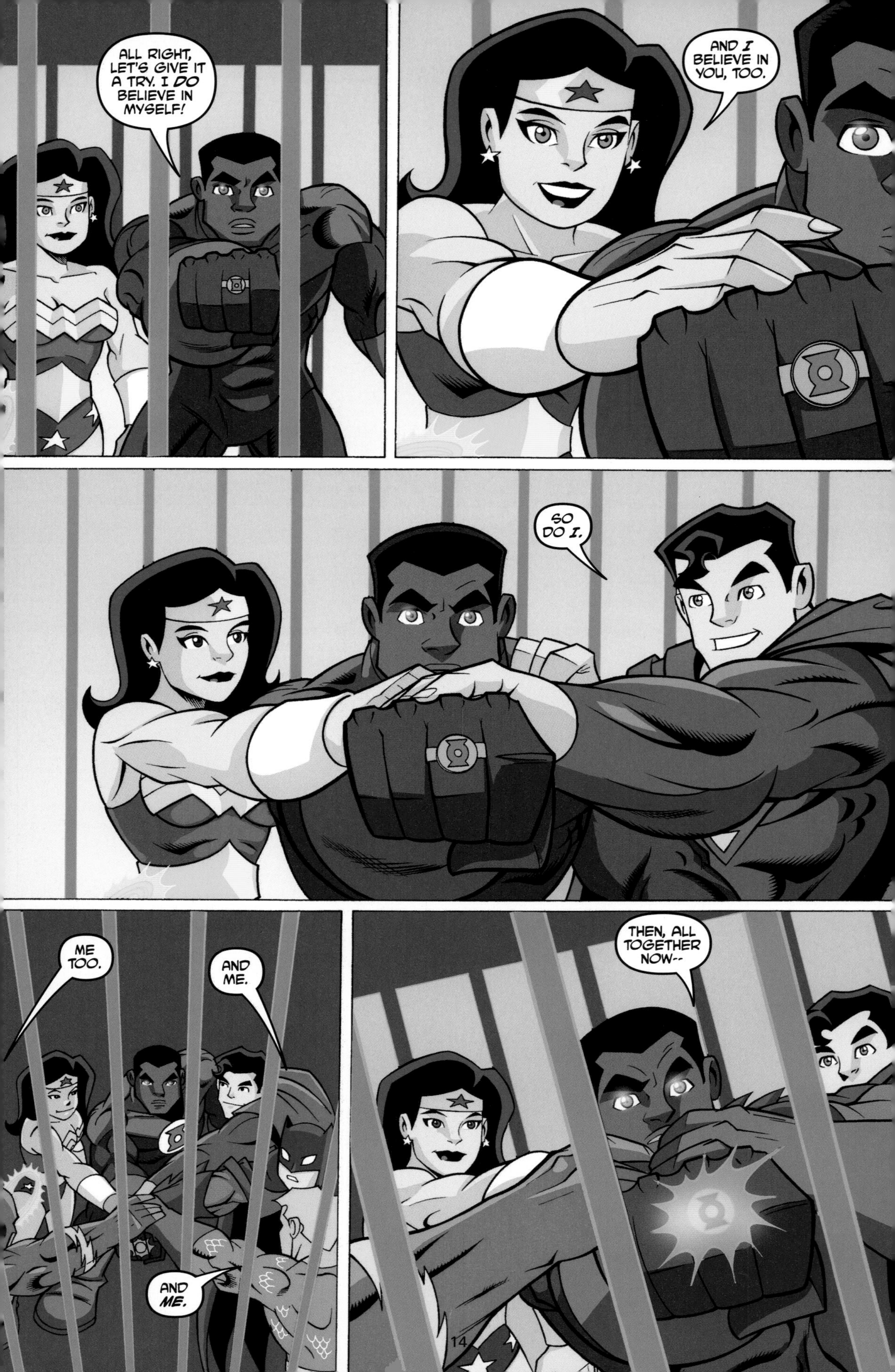
ALL RIGHT, LET'S GIVE IT A TRY. I *DO* BELIEVE IN MYSELF!
AND *I* BELIEVE IN YOU, TOO.
SO DO *I*.
ME TOO.
AND ME.
AND *ME.*
THEN, ALL TOGETHER NOW--

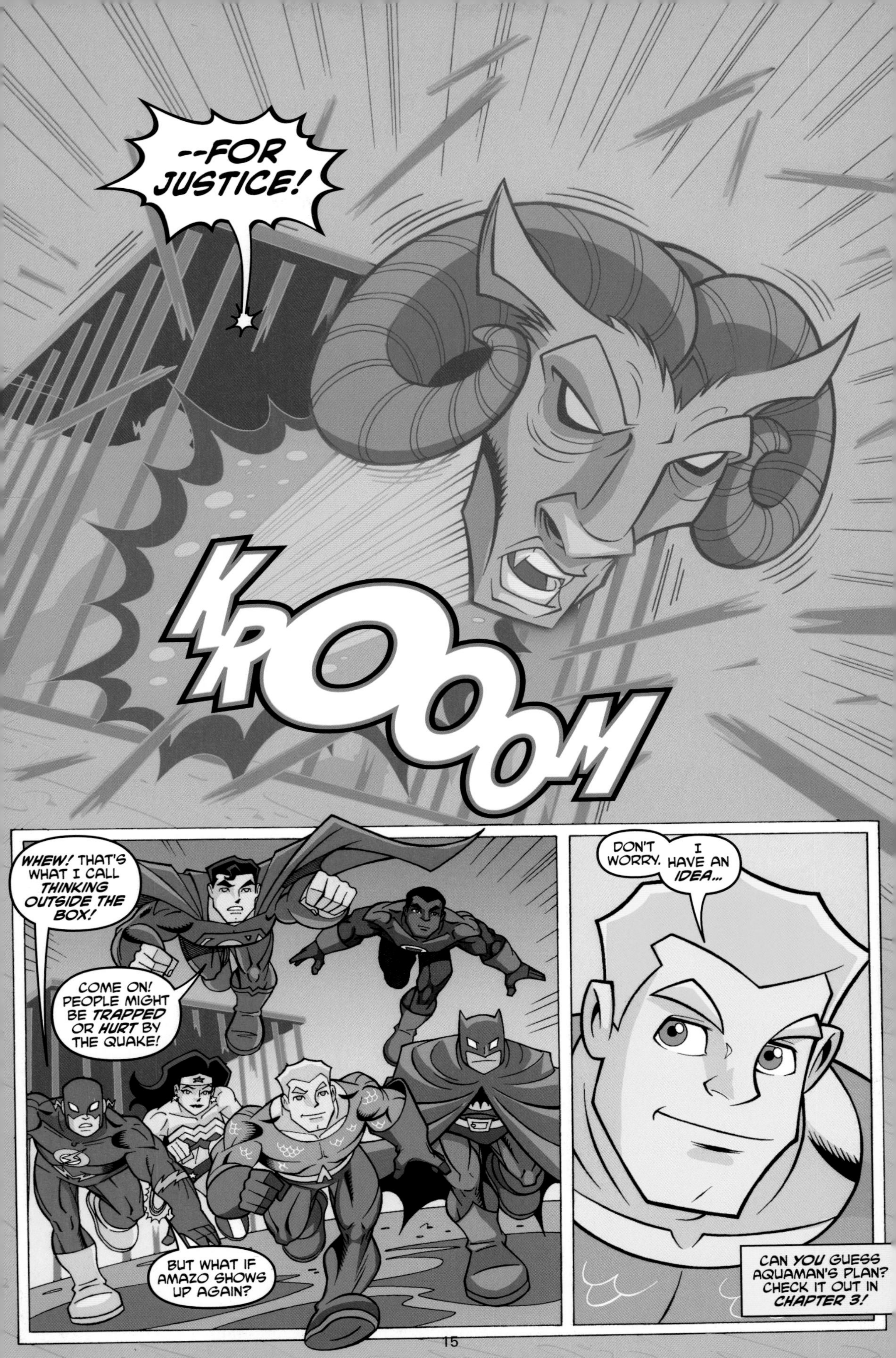
--FOR JUSTICE!
KROOOOM
WHEW! THAT'S WHAT I CALL THINKING OUTSIDE THE BOX!
COME ON! PEOPLE MIGHT BE TRAPPED OR HURT BY THE QUAKE!
BUT WHAT IF AMAZO SHOWS UP AGAIN?
DON'T WORRY.
I HAVE AN IDEA...
CAN YOU GUESS AQUAMAN'S PLAN? CHECK IT OUT IN CHAPTER 3!

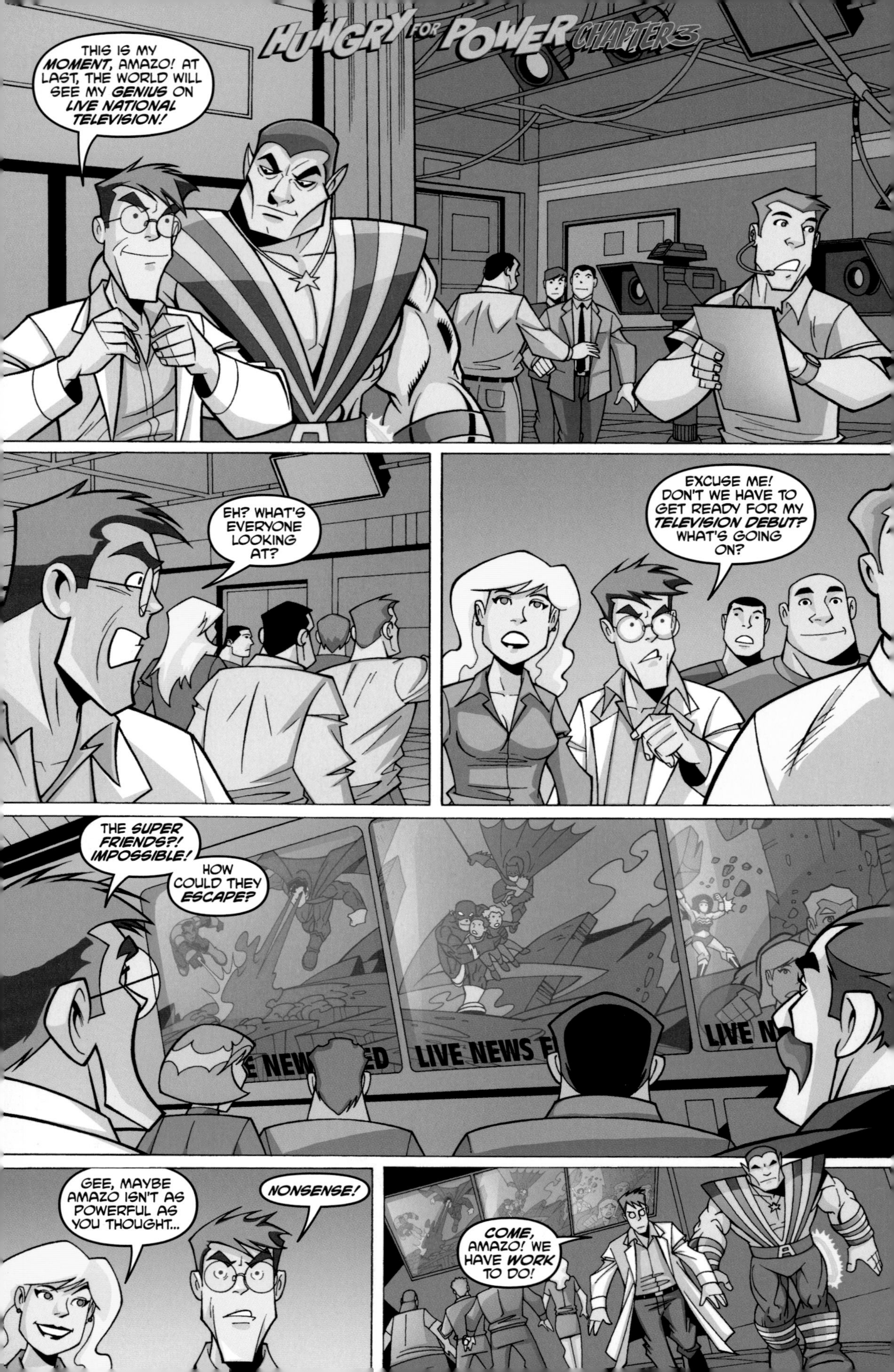
HUNGRY FOR POWER CHAPTER 3
THIS IS MY MOMENT, AMAZO! AT LAST, THE WORLD WILL SEE MY GENIUS ON LIVE NATIONAL TELEVISION!
EH? WHAT'S EVERYONE LOOKING AT?
EXCUSE ME! DON'T WE HAVE TO GET READY FOR MY TELEVISION DEBUT? WHAT'S GOING ON?
THE SUPER FRIENDS?! IMPOSSIBLE!
HOW COULD THEY ESCAPE?
LIVE NEWS FEED
GEE, MAYBE AMAZO ISN'T AS POWERFUL AS YOU THOUGHT...
NONSENSE!
COME, AMAZO! WE HAVE WORK TO DO!

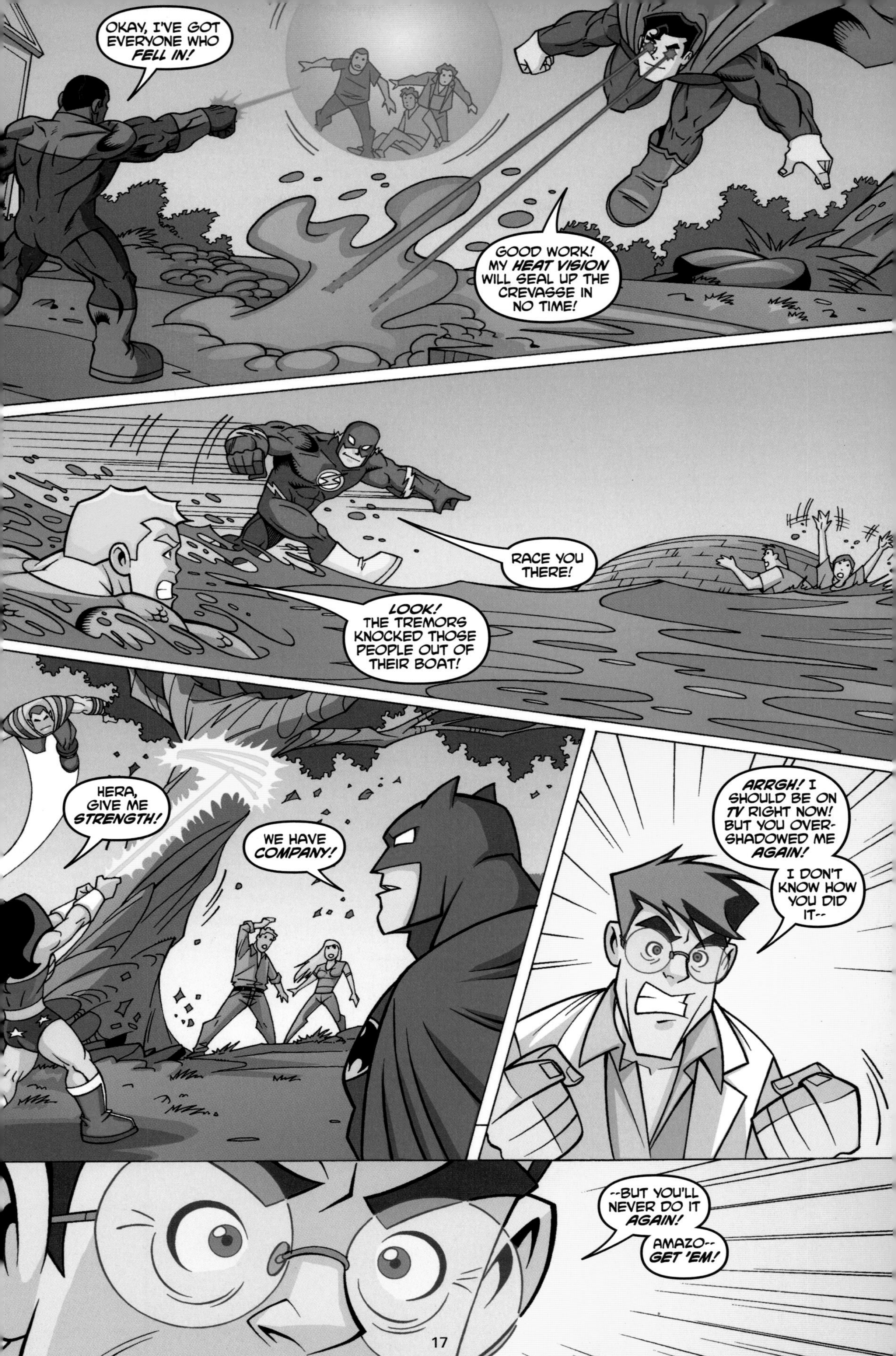
OKAY, I'VE GOT EVERYONE WHO FELL IN!
GOOD WORK! MY HEAT VISION WILL SEAL UP THE CREVASSE IN NO TIME!
RACE YOU THERE!
LOOK! THE TREMORS KNOCKED THOSE PEOPLE OUT OF THEIR BOAT!
HERA, GIVE ME STRENGTH!
WE HAVE COMPANY!
ARRGH! I SHOULD BE ON TV RIGHT NOW! BUT YOU OVER-SHADOWED ME AGAIN!
I DON'T KNOW HOW YOU DID IT--
--BUT YOU'LL NEVER DO IT AGAIN!
AMAZO-- GET 'EM!

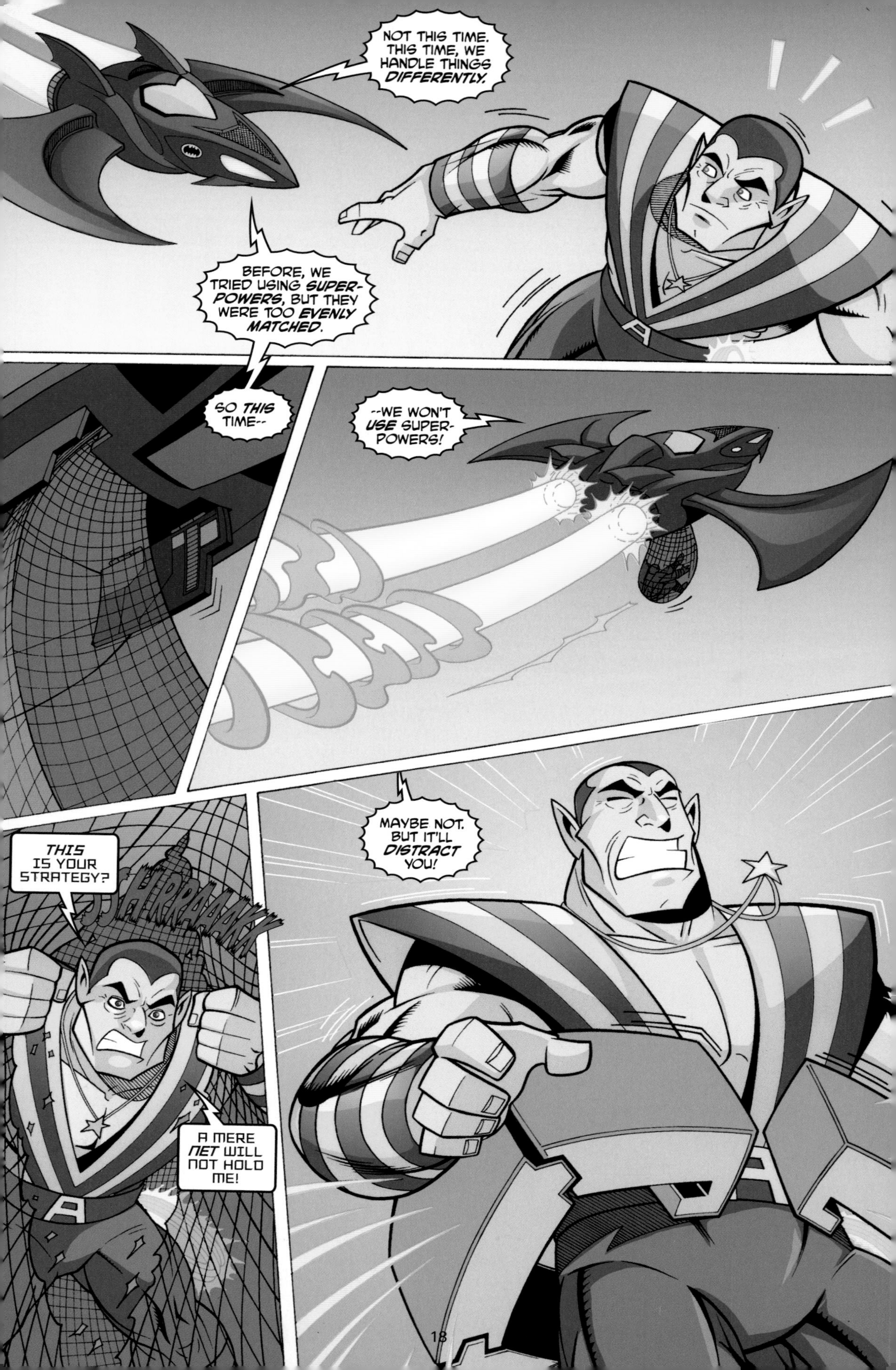
NOT THIS TIME. THIS TIME, WE HANDLE THINGS *DIFFERENTLY.*
BEFORE, WE TRIED USING *SUPER-POWERS*, BUT THEY WERE TOO *EVENLY MATCHED*.
SO *THIS* TIME--
--WE WON'T *USE* SUPER-POWERS!
*THIS* IS YOUR STRATEGY?
A MERE *NET* WILL NOT HOLD ME!
MAYBE NOT. BUT IT'LL *DISTRACT* YOU!

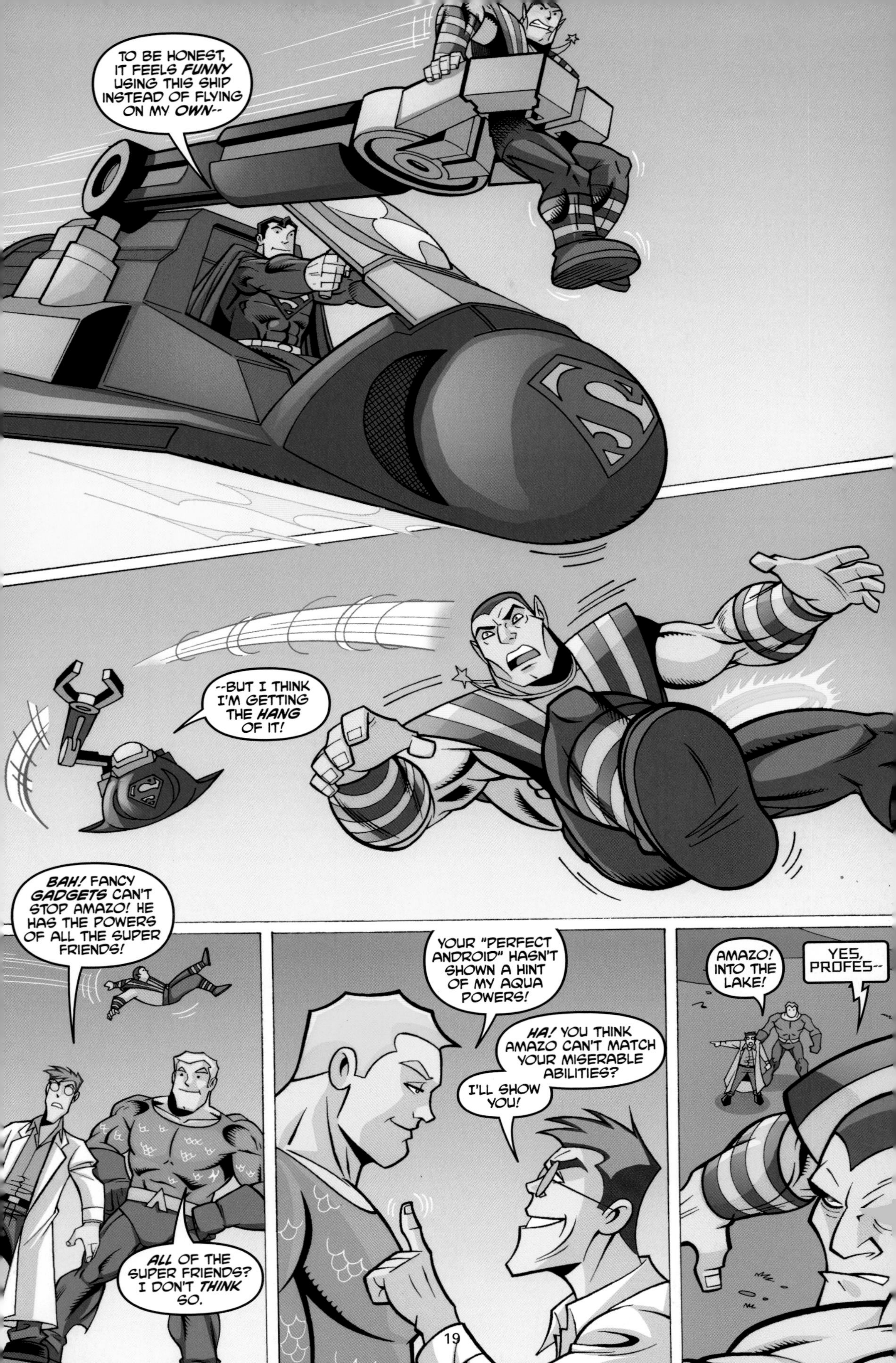

TO BE HONEST, IT FEELS FUNNY USING THIS SHIP INSTEAD OF FLYING ON MY OWN--
--BUT I THINK I'M GETTING THE HANG OF IT!
BAH! FANCY GADGETS CAN'T STOP AMAZO! HE HAS THE POWERS OF ALL THE SUPER FRIENDS!
ALL OF THE SUPER FRIENDS? I DON'T THINK SO.
YOUR "PERFECT ANDROID" HASN'T SHOWN A HINT OF MY AQUA POWERS!
HA! YOU THINK AMAZO CAN'T MATCH YOUR MISERABLE ABILITIES?
I'LL SHOW YOU!
AMAZO! INTO THE LAKE!
YES, PROFES--

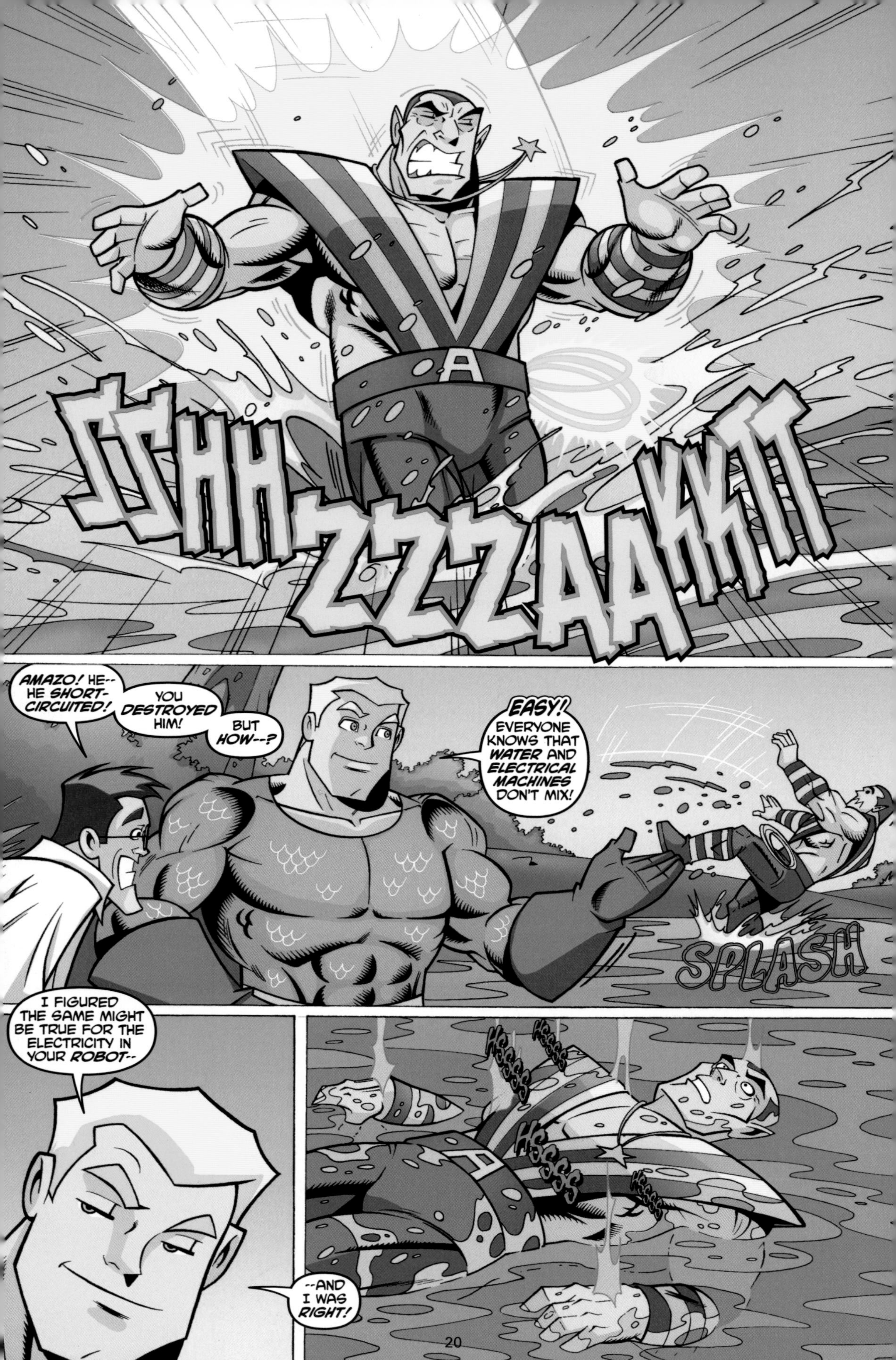
SSHH-ZZZAAKKTT
AMAZO! HE-- HE SHORT-CIRCUITED!
YOU DESTROYED HIM!
BUT HOW--?
EASY! EVERYONE KNOWS THAT WATER AND ELECTRICAL MACHINES DON'T MIX!
SPLASH
I FIGURED THE SAME MIGHT BE TRUE FOR THE ELECTRICITY IN YOUR ROBOT--
HSSSS
HSSSS
HSSSS
HSSSS
HSSSS
--AND I WAS RIGHT!

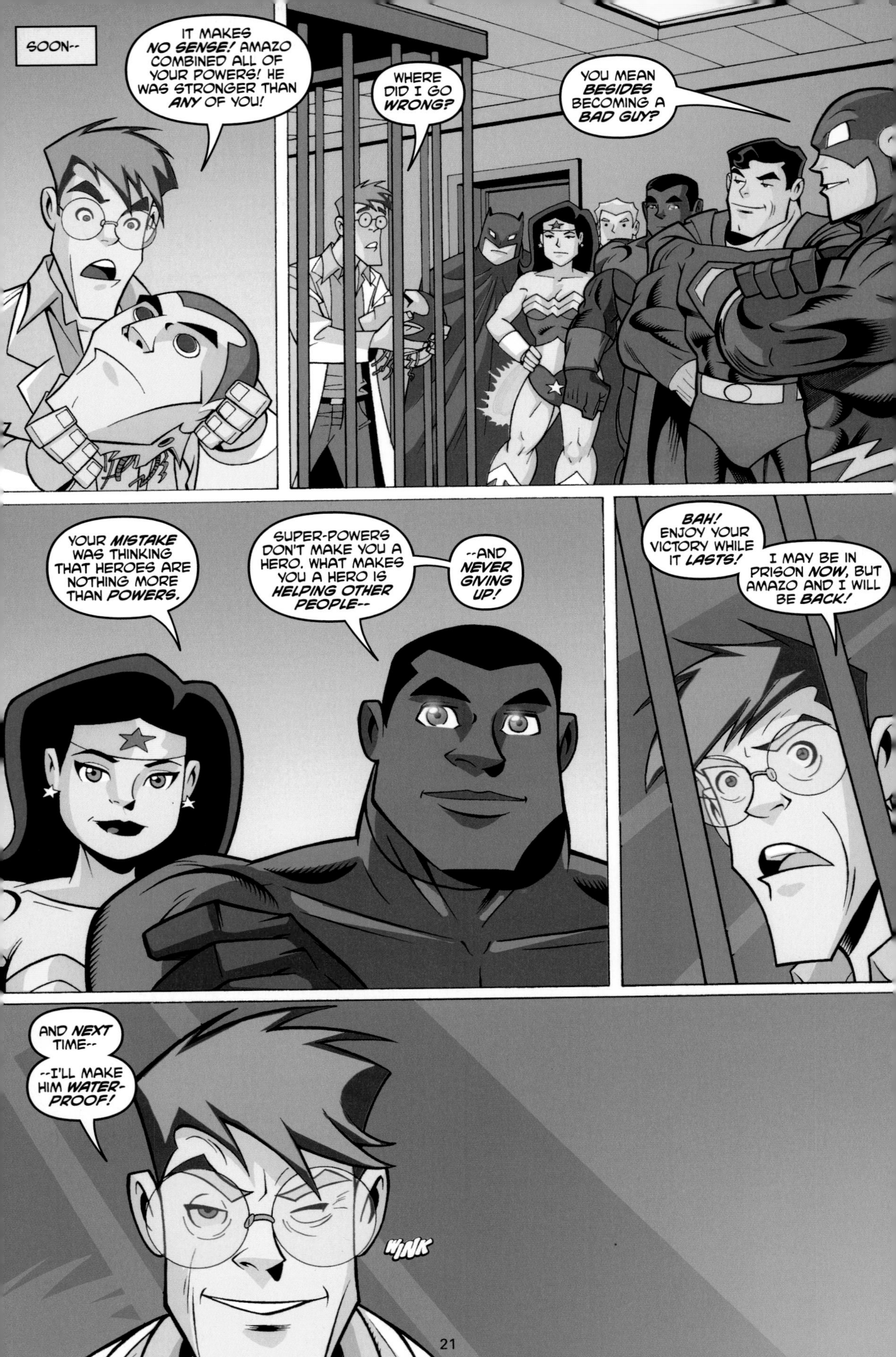
SOON--
IT MAKES NO SENSE! AMAZO COMBINED ALL OF YOUR POWERS! HE WAS STRONGER THAN ANY OF YOU!
WHERE DID I GO WRONG?
YOU MEAN BESIDES BECOMING A BAD GUY?
YOUR MISTAKE WAS THINKING THAT HEROES ARE NOTHING MORE THAN POWERS.
SUPER-POWERS DON'T MAKE YOU A HERO. WHAT MAKES YOU A HERO IS HELPING OTHER PEOPLE--
--AND NEVER GIVING UP!
BAH! ENJOY YOUR VICTORY WHILE IT LASTS!
I MAY BE IN PRISON NOW, BUT AMAZO AND I WILL BE BACK!
AND NEXT TIME--
--I'LL MAKE HIM WATER-PROOF!
WINK

# ATTENTION, ALL SUPER FRIENDS!

HERE'S THIS BOOK'S SECRET MESSAGE:

**PEVOY CYSOXRP ZBBU BEI CBY BINOYP**

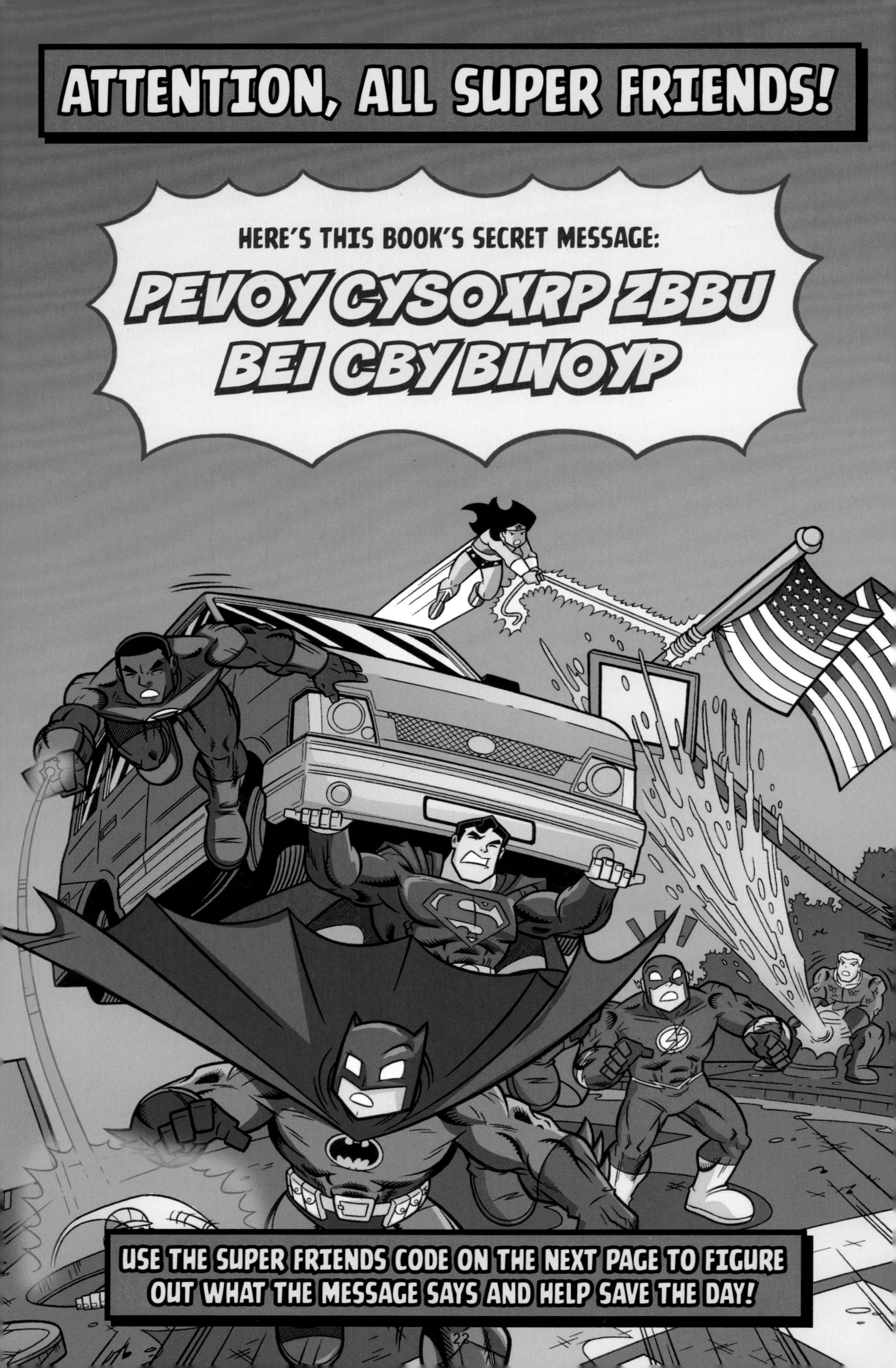

USE THE SUPER FRIENDS CODE ON THE NEXT PAGE TO FIGURE OUT WHAT THE MESSAGE SAYS AND HELP SAVE THE DAY!

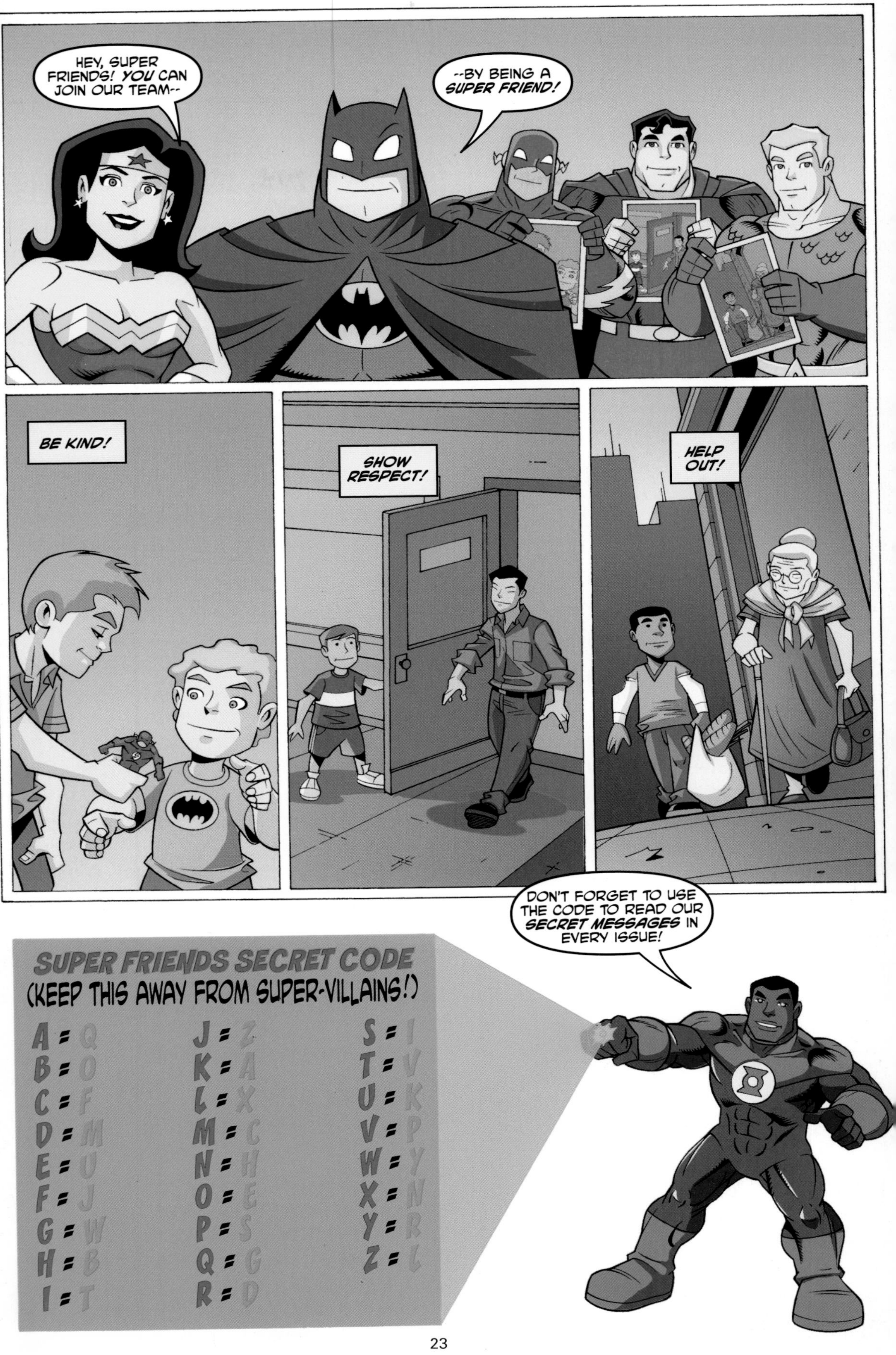
HEY, SUPER FRIENDS! YOU CAN JOIN OUR TEAM--
--BY BEING A SUPER FRIEND!
BE KIND!
SHOW RESPECT!
HELP OUT!
DON'T FORGET TO USE THE CODE TO READ OUR SECRET MESSAGES IN EVERY ISSUE!
SUPER FRIENDS SECRET CODE
(KEEP THIS AWAY FROM SUPER-VILLAINS!)
A = Q
B = O
C = F
D = M
E = U
F = J
G = W
H = B
I = T
J = Z
K = A
L = X
M = C
N = H
O = E
P = S
Q = G
R = D
S = I
T = V
U = K
V = P
W = Y
X = N
Y = R
Z = L

# KNOW YOUR SUPER FRIENDS!

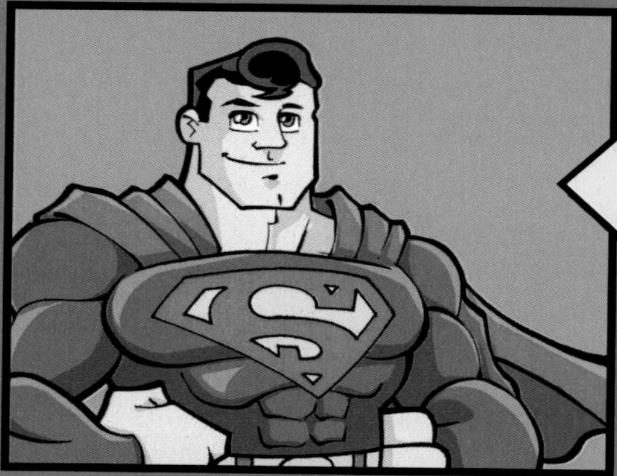

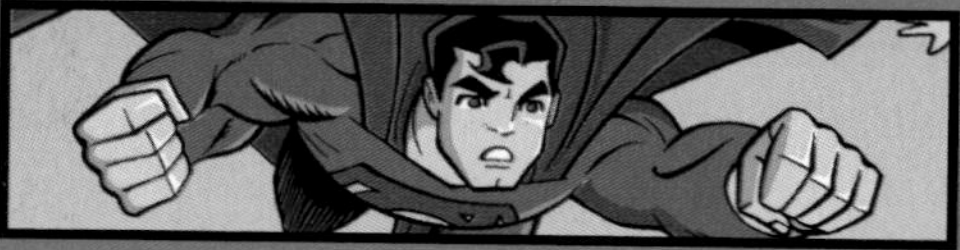

## SUPERMAN

**Real Name:** Clark Kent

**Powers:** Super-strength, super-speed, flight, super-senses, heat vision, invulnerability, super-breath

**Origin:** Just before the planet Krypton exploded, baby Kal-EL escaped in a rocket to Earth. On Earth, he was adopted by a kind couple named Jonathan and Martha Kent.

## BATMAN

**Secret Identity:** Bruce Wayne

**Abilities:** World's greatest detective, acrobat, escape artist

**Origin:** Orphaned at a young age, young millionaire Bruce Wayne promised to keep all people safe from crime. After training for many years, he put on costume that would scare criminals - the costume of Batman.

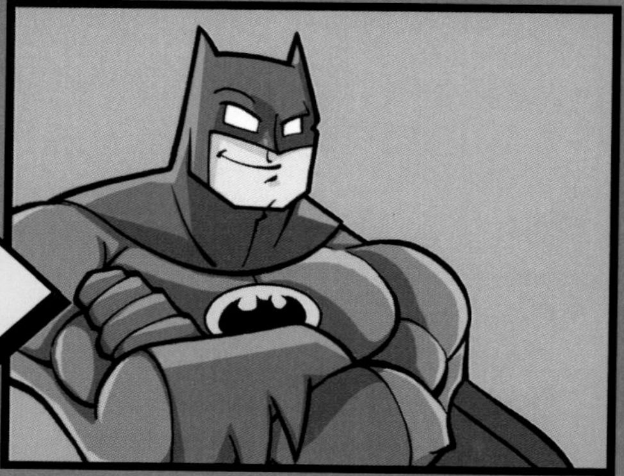

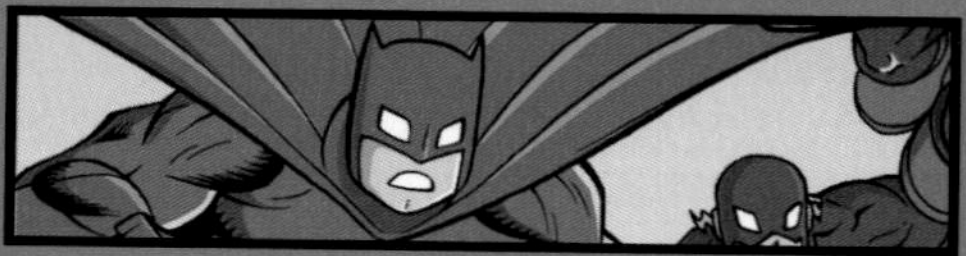

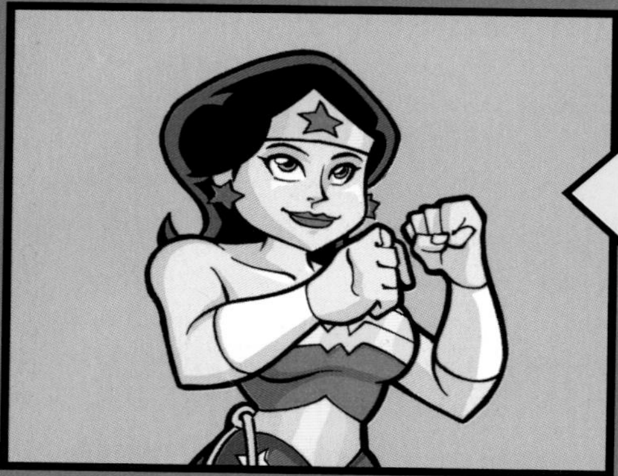

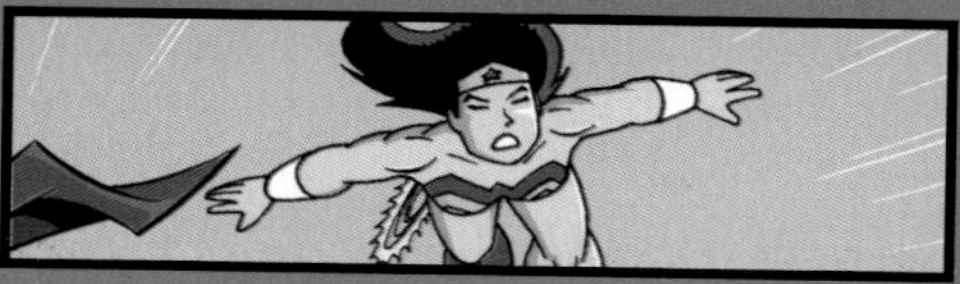

## WONDER WOMAN

**Secret Identity:** Princess Diana

**Powers:** Super-strong, faster than normal humans, uses her bracelets as shields and magic lasso to make people tell the truth

**Origin:** Diana is the Princess of Paradise Island, the hidden home of the Amazons. When Diana was a baby, the Greek gods gave her special powers.

# GREEN LANTERN

**Secret Identity:** John Stewart

**Powers:** Through the strength of willpower, Green Lantern's power ring can create anything he imagines

**Origin:** Led by the Guardians of the Universe, the Green Lantern Corps is an outer-space police force that keeps the whole universe safe. The Guardians chose John to protect Earth as our planet's Green Lantern.

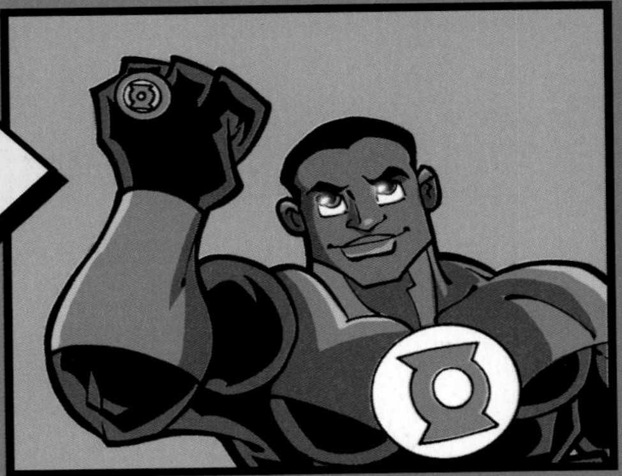

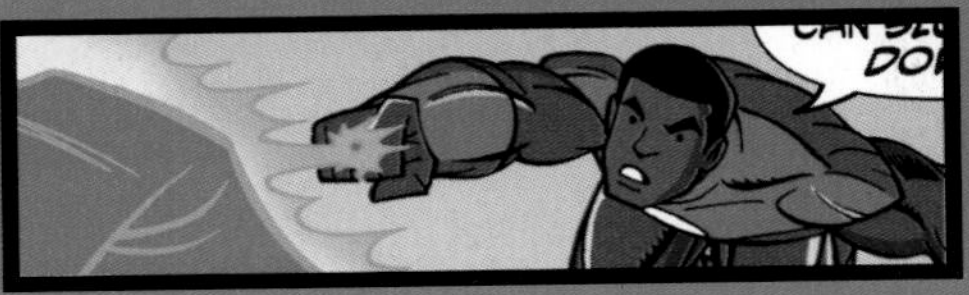

# THE FLASH

**Secret Identity:** Wally West

**Powers:** Flash uses his super-speed in many ways: he can run across water or up the side of a building, spin around to make a tornado, or vibrate his body to walk right through a wall

**Origin:** As a boy, Wally West became the super-fast Kid Flash when lightning hit a rack of chemicals that spilled on him. Today, he helps others as the Flash.

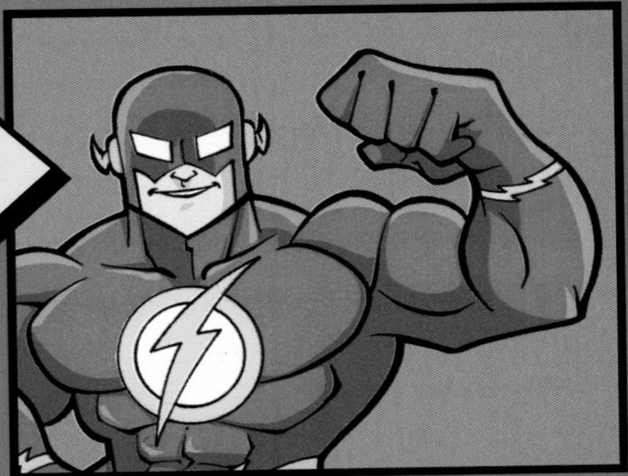

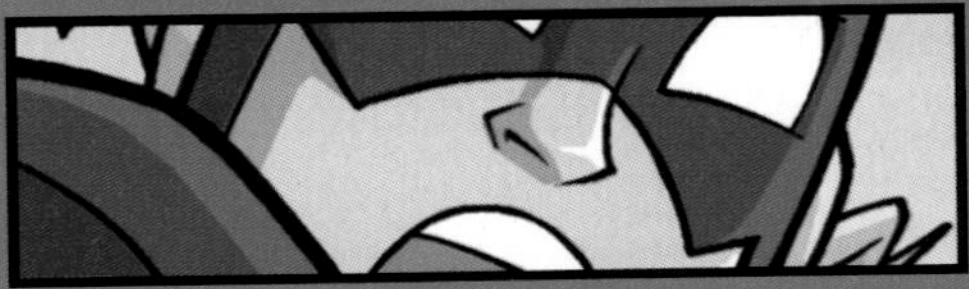

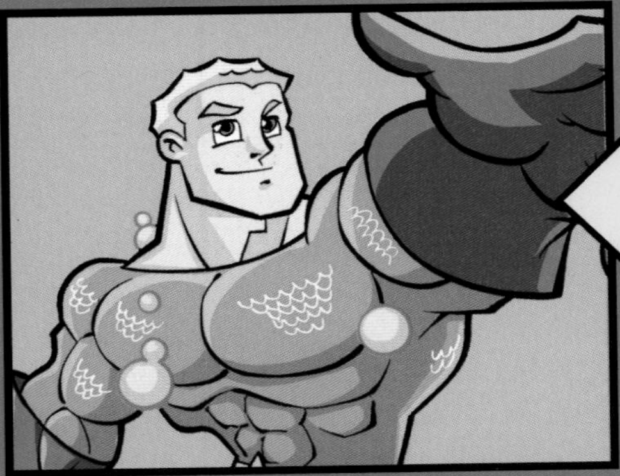

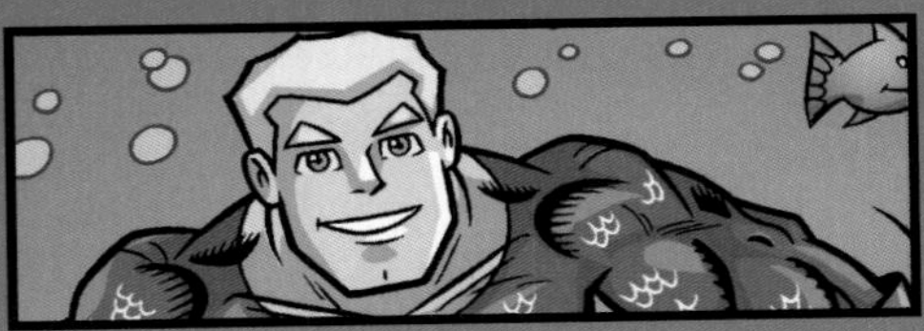

# AQUAMAN

**Real Name:** King Orin or Arthur Curry

**Powers:** Breathes underwater, communicates with fish, swims at high speed, stronger than normal humans

**Origin:** Orin's father was a lighthouse keeper and his mother was a mermaid from the undersea land of Atlantis. As Orin grew up, he learned that he could live on land and underwater. He decided to use his powers to keep the seven seas safe as Aquaman.

# CREATORS

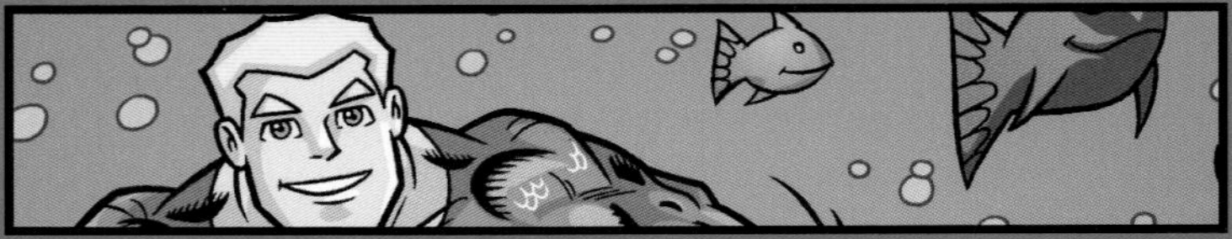

## SHOLLY FISCH WRITER

Bitten by a radioactive typewriter, Sholly Fisch has spent the wee hours writing books, comics, TV scripts, and online material for more than 25 years. His comic book credits include more than 200 stories and features about characters such as Batman, Superman, Bugs Bunny, Daffy Duck, Spider-Man, and Ben 10. Currently, he writes stories for Action Comics every month, plus stories for Looney Tunes and Scooby-Doo. By day, Sholly is a mild-mannered developmental psychologist who helps to create educational TV shows, web sites, and other media for kids.

## DARIO BRIZUELA ARTIST

Dario Brizuela is a professional comic book artist. He's illustrated some of today's most popular characters, including Batman, Green Lantern, Teenage Mutant Ninja Turtles, Thor, Iron Man, and Transformers. His best-known works for DC Comics include the series DC Super Friends, Justice League Unlimited, and Batman: The Brave and the Bold.

## J. BONE COVER ARTIST

J.Bone is a Toronto based illustrator and comic book artist. Besides DC Super Friends, he has worked on comic books such as Spiderman: Tangled Web, Mr. Gum, Gotham Girls, and Madman Adventures. He is also the co-creator of the Alison Dare comic book series.

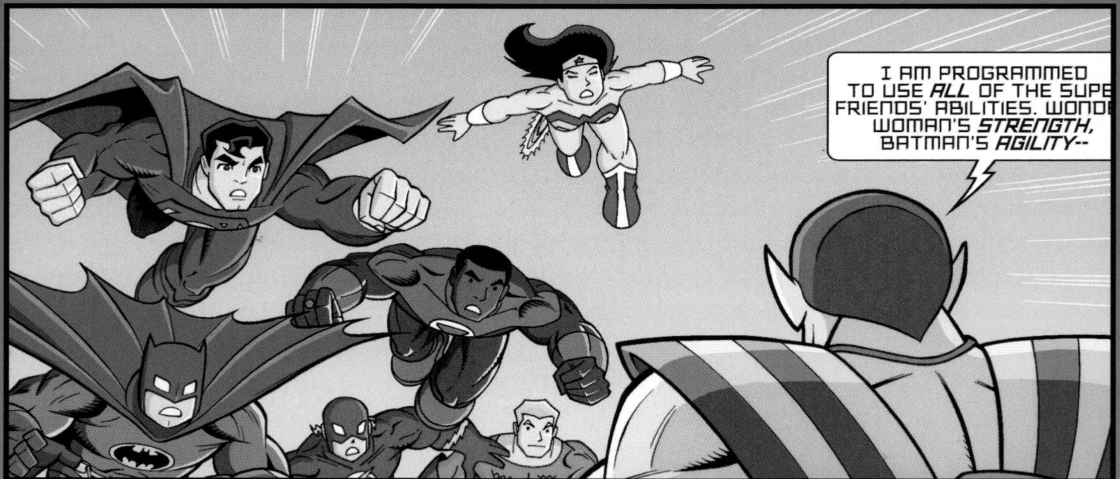
I AM PROGRAMMED TO USE ALL OF THE SUPE FRIENDS' ABILITIES. WONDE WOMAN'S STRENGTH, BATMAN'S AGILITY--

# GLOSSARY

**abilities** [uh·BIL·i·tees]-powers to do something

**agility** [uh·JIL·i·tee]-the power to move quickly and easily

**cavern** [KAV·ern]-a large cave

**convinced** [kuhn·VINSSD]-made someone believe something

**debut** [DAY·byoo]-a first public appearance

**dense** [DENSS]-thick, or crowded

**distract** [diss·TRAKT]-to draw the attention or mind to something else

**earthquake** [URTH·kwayk]-a sudden, violent shaking of the Earth caused by a shifting of the Earth's crust

**experience** [ek·SPEER·ee·uhnss]-the knowledge and skill that you gain by doing something

**genius** [JEE·nee·uhss]-an unusually intelligent or talented person

**miserable** [MIZ·ur·uh·buhl]-sad, unhappy, or dejected

**permanent** [PUR·muh·nuhnt]-lasting, or meant to last for a long time

**robotics** [roh·BOT·iks]-the study of making and using robots

**strategy** [STRAT·uh·jee]-a clever plan for winning a battle or achieving a goal

**tremors** [TREM·urs]-a shaking or trembling movement

**vibrate** [VYE·brate]-to move back and forth rapidly

**willpower** [wihl·POU·ur]-the power to choose or control what you will and will not do

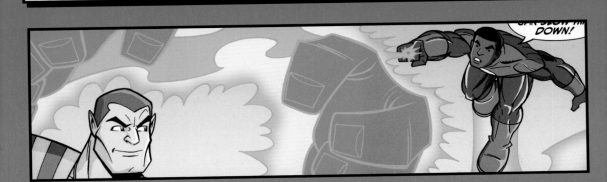

# VISUAL QUESTIONS & PROMPTS

**1.** Professor Ivo is a robotics scientist. In this image, we see one example of his inventions. What is it? What other sort of inventions might a robotics scientist create?

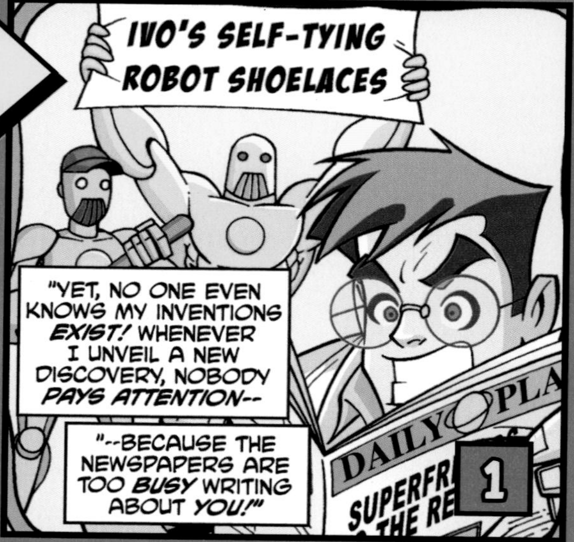

IVO'S SELF-TYING ROBOT SHOELACES
"YET, NO ONE EVEN KNOWS MY INVENTIONS *EXIST!* WHENEVER I UNVEIL A NEW DISCOVERY, NOBODY *PAYS ATTENTION*--
"--BECAUSE THE NEWSPAPERS ARE TOO *BUSY* WRITING ABOUT *YOU!*"
1


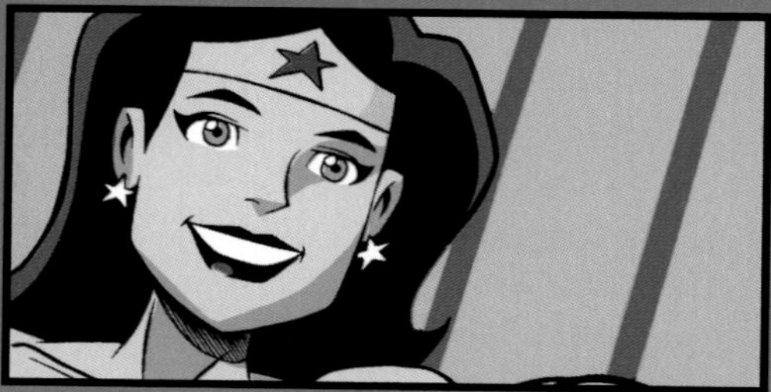

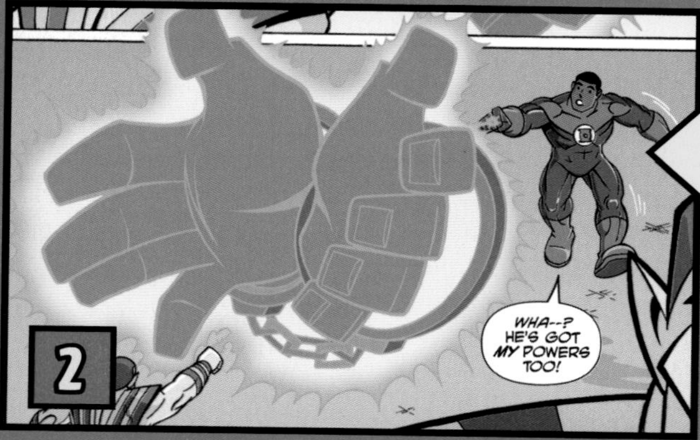

WHA--? HE'S GOT *MY* POWERS TOO!
2


**2.** How do we know when the Green Lantern is using his power ring? What visual clues do you see?

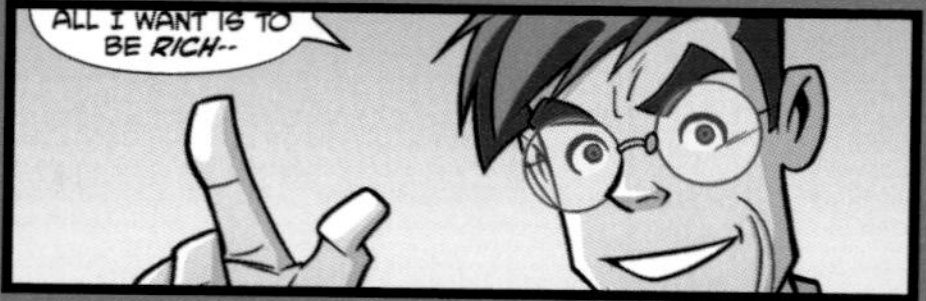

ALL I WANT IS TO BE *RICH*--


**3.** Amazo has the powers of all the super heroes. Whose superpower does he use to create the cage that holds all the heroes [see panels at right]? How do you know?

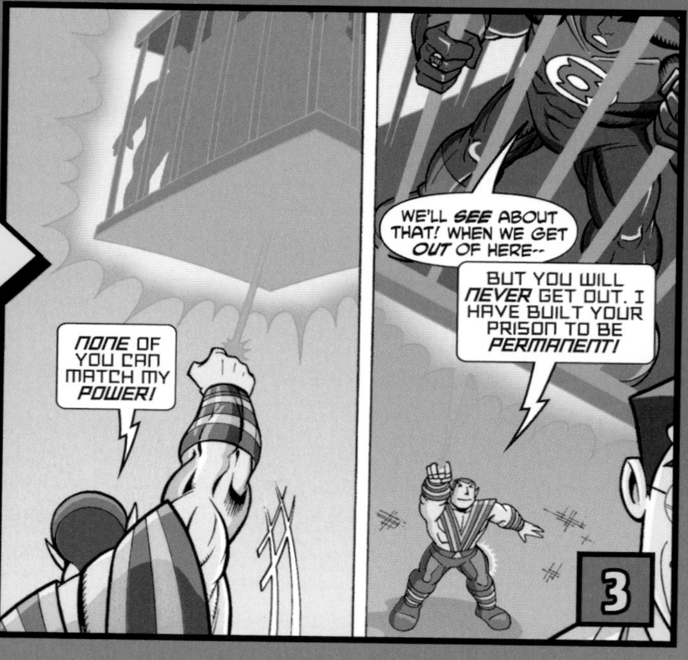

*NONE* OF YOU CAN MATCH MY *POWER!*
WE'LL *SEE* ABOUT THAT! WHEN WE GET *OUT* OF HERE--
BUT YOU WILL *NEVER* GET OUT. I HAVE BUILT YOUR PRISON TO BE *PERMANENT!*
3


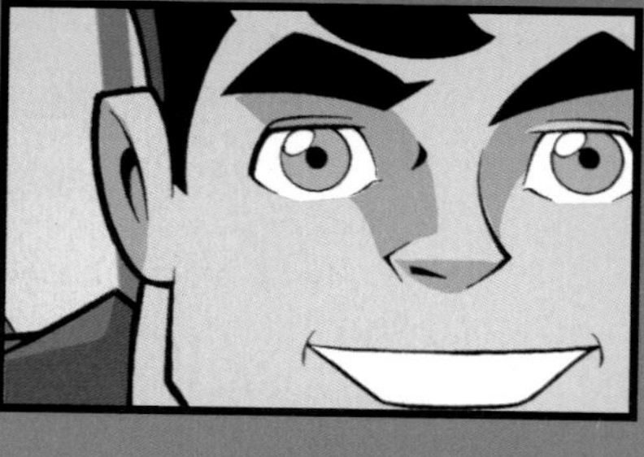

**4.** What is happening in this panel? How do we know?

**4**

--UM, GUYS? IS THIS PART OF THE PLAN...?

RRRUUUMMMMMBBLLLLLL

**5.** In this panel, we find out what the super heroes are doing, even though this part of the story follows Dr. Ivo. What are the heroes doing? How does Dr. Ivo feel about this? Why?

THE SUPER FRIENDS?! IMPOSSIBLE!

HOW COULD THEY ESCAPE?

LIVE NEWS F

**5**

**6.** Explain what the boys in this series of panels are doing to be Super Friends.

BE KIND!

SHOW RESPECT!

HELP OUT!

**6**

# READ THEM ALL!

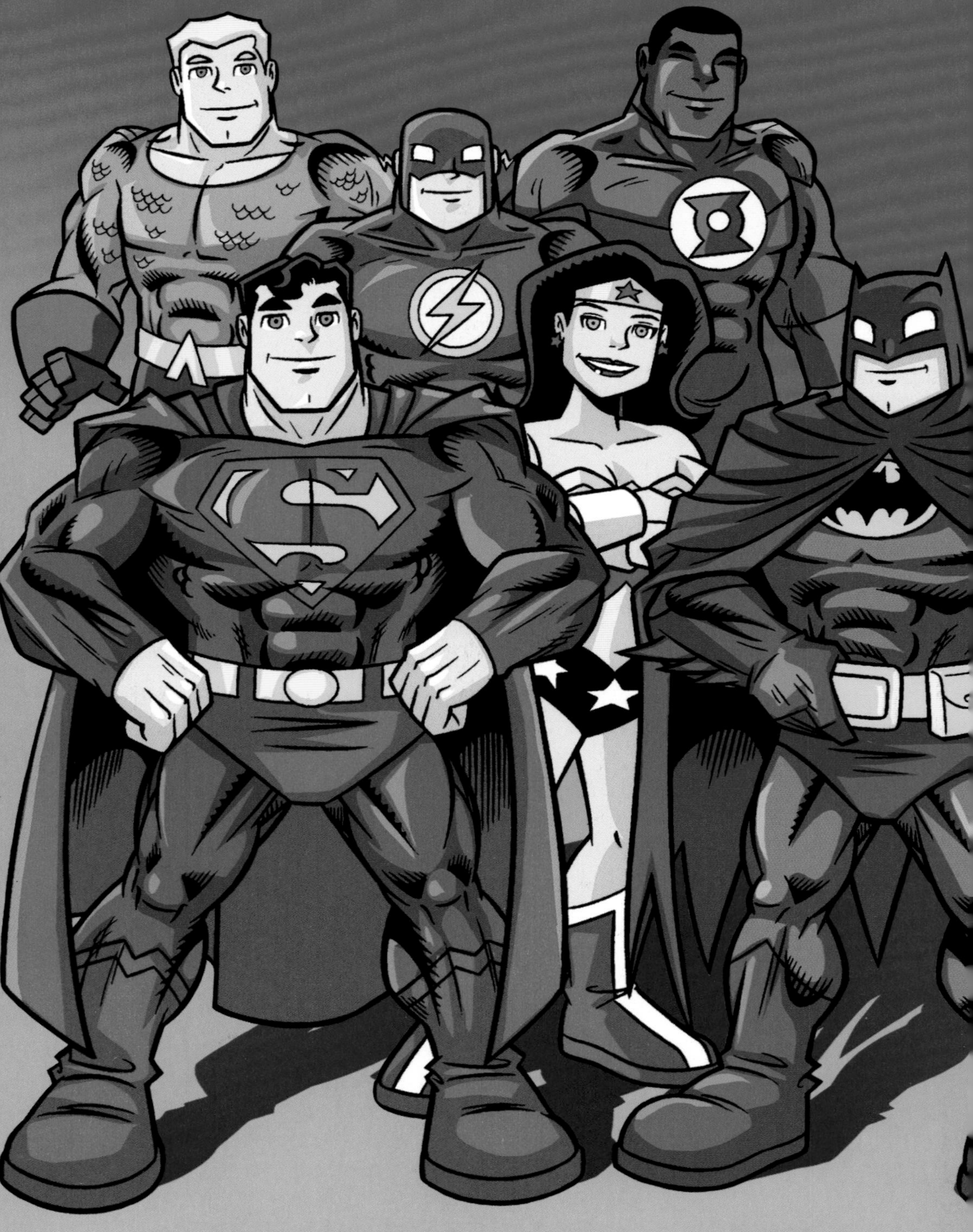

# DC SUPER FRIENDS™

DC COMICS
DC SUPER FRIENDS
HUNGRY FOR POWER
Fisch • Brizuela

Hungry for Power

DC COMICS
DC SUPER FRIENDS
DINOSAUR ROUND-UP
Fisch • Ottolini • Staton

Dinosaur Round-up

DC COMICS
DC SUPER FRIENDS
WANTED: THE SUPER FRIENDS
Fisch • McKenny • Moy

Wanted: The Super Friends

DC COMICS
DC SUPER FRIENDS
APRIL FOOLS
Fisch • Brizuela

April Fools

**ONLY FROM...**

**STONE ARCH BOOKS™**

a capstone imprint www.capstonepub.com

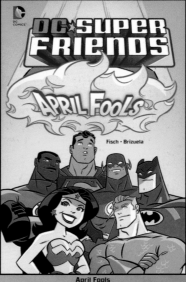

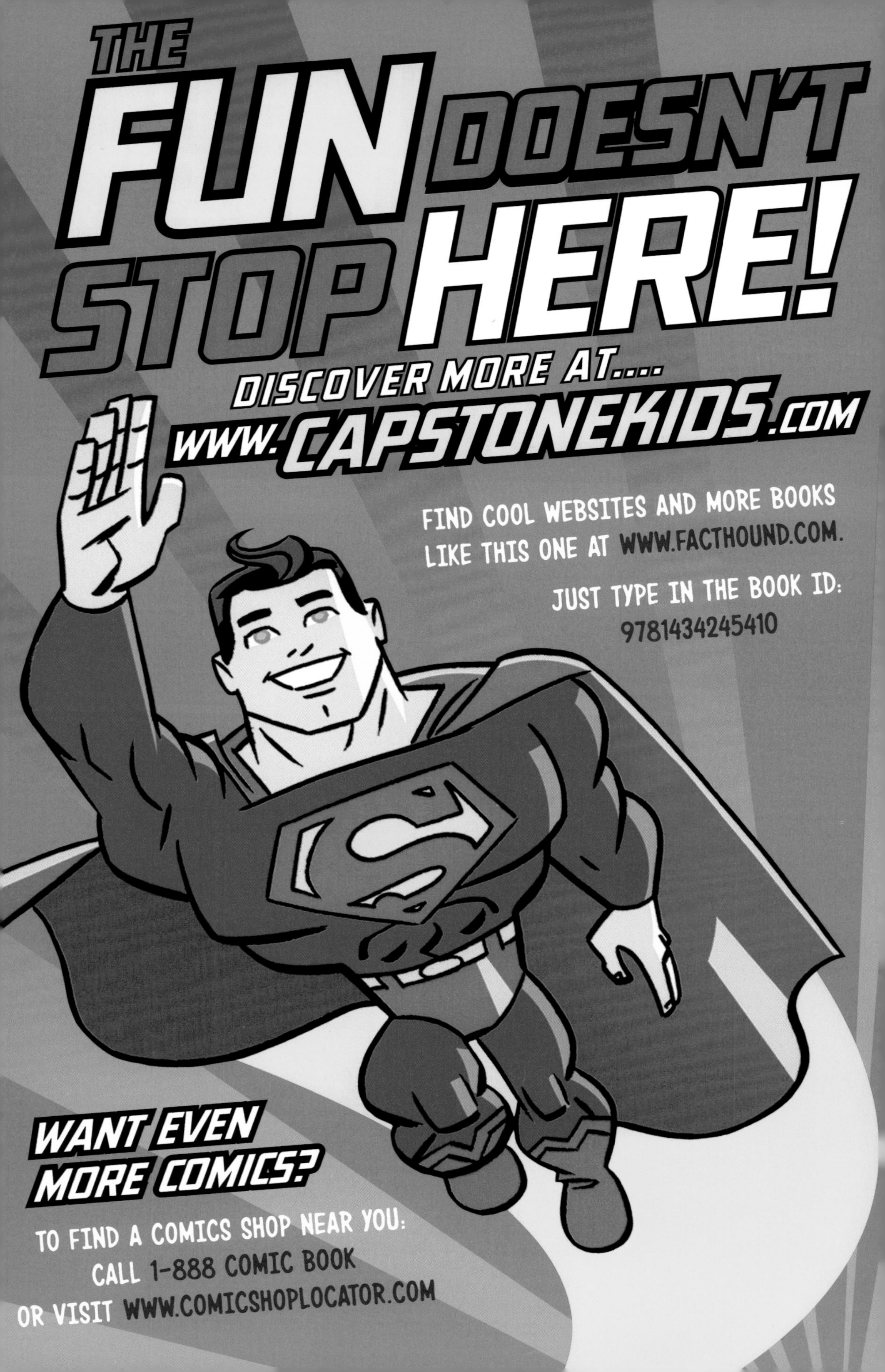
THE FUN DOESN'T STOP HERE!
DISCOVER MORE AT....
WWW.CAPSTONEKIDS.COM
FIND COOL WEBSITES AND MORE BOOKS LIKE THIS ONE AT WWW.FACTHOUND.COM.
JUST TYPE IN THE BOOK ID:
9781434245410
WANT EVEN MORE COMICS?
TO FIND A COMICS SHOP NEAR YOU:
CALL 1-888 COMIC BOOK
OR VISIT WWW.COMICSHOPLOCATOR.COM